DARK SECRETS
A DARK BLADE PREQUEL NOVELLA
TYREAN MARTINSON

CONTENTS

Chapter I: A Gathering of Nobles

DAN TORREN STOOD NEAR the great marble pillars at the edge of the crowded hall, his fingers tracing the rim of a half-full goblet. The celebration of Septily's unification had brought together nobles, courtiers, and members of the Triune Halls from all seven formerly independent kingdoms. Bright tapestries draped every wall, each bearing the sigils of the united realms, while glittering chandeliers cast a golden glow over the throngs of attendees

He shifted on his feet, adjusting the ceremonial sword hanging at his side. Its weight felt wrong tonight, as if it didn't belong to him. Not that it mattered. He hadn't drawn it in weeks, not since Thorn—his Sword Guard and mentor—had vanished from the Torren estate.

Dan's fingers tightened on the goblet. He still didn't know where Thorn had gone, or why his parents refused to give him any real answers about the disappearance. His father had brushed off his concerns with vague mentions of "important duties," while his mother had coldly suggested that perhaps Thorn wasn't as loyal as he appeared. Neither of them cared that Thorn had been more than just a trainer to Dan—he had been a mentor, a guide, someone who treated Dan as more than a pawn in the endless game of noble politics.

And now, he was gone.

Dan swallowed against the knot in his throat and forced himself to take in the scene around him. Sword Guards in their distinctive silver, black, and gray uniforms mingled with the guests and stood at attention near the exits, their watchful eyes scanning for any sign of trouble. Shepherds, easily identifiable by their green or brown robes and the silver pendants hanging from their necks, moved through the crowd, offering words of wisdom and comfort to those who sought it. And there, near the center of the room, a group of Lawgivers huddled in deep discussion, their navy blue and gold attire a reflection of their connection to the royal family, though less ornate than the regalia of true royalty.

This gathering was meant to celebrate unity, but Dan could feel the undercurrents of tension beneath the surface. Although the unity of their country had taken place ages ago, many of the nobles worked against one another, vying for more power.

His eyes flicked to a group near the center of the hall. There, surrounded by admirers and sycophants, stood Prince Alex.

Dan's stomach twisted.

Alex looked every bit the part of a prince—tall, confident, dressed in deep navy with gold trim that caught the light. He smiled and laughed with those around him, as if the entire court had been gathered just to bask in his presence. And perhaps, in a way, they had. Alex was the crown prince, the future king. His every word was scrutinized, every action noted. He carried the weight of expectation as effortlessly as if it were a light mantle draped over his shoulders.

Dan couldn't help but feel a pang of something—bitterness? Regret? He wasn't sure. Once, long ago, they had been friends. True friends. Before the world had become so complicated, before politics and loyalty had driven a wedge between them, Alex had been one of the few people Dan could trust.

They'd grown up together, practically inseparable as boys. Dan could still remember the days when they would pretend to be legendary heroes, swearing oaths of eternal brotherhood as if the blood in their veins wasn't noble but something pure and unbreakable. Back then, they hadn't cared about rank or titles. They'd been equals.

But that was before.

Dan's jaw clenched as he recalled the conversation with his mother earlier that day.

"Pay attention to Prince Alex tonight," she had said, her tone clipped, her eyes sharp. "Find out who he's speaking to, what he's planning. His father may be the King, but Alex is still just a boy, vulnerable to... influence. We need to know where his loyalties lie."

She hadn't said it outright, but Dan knew what she meant. Find something—anything—that could be used as leverage against the prince. The very idea made his skin crawl. He hadn't wanted to come to this gathering, hadn't wanted to be part of their schemes, but his parents had given him little choice.

Dan's father had been less subtle. "This is about securing our family's future," Lord Torren had said, his voice as cold as iron. "We can't afford to be sentimental. Do what needs to be done."

Dan's gaze lingered on Alex across the hall, and a wave of frustration washed over him. He couldn't do it. How could they expect him to betray the boy who had once been his best friend? The boy who had stood by his side through countless childhood scrapes, who had defended him from bullies, who had promised they would always look out for each other?

Dan drained the rest of his wine and set the goblet down on a nearby table, his jaw tight with anger. It wasn't just his parents' demands that ate at him—it was the silence around Thorn's disappearance. It had been weeks now, and every time Dan asked about his mentor, he was met with deflection. Thorn wasn't the type to just vanish without a word. He was a man of honor—but more than that, Thorn had always been straight with Dan, never keeping secrets.

Something was wrong. Deeply wrong.

The memory of his last conversation with Thorn played in his mind. They had been in the training yard, locked in a grueling sword drill. Thorn had been pushing him harder than usual, his strikes fast and relentless. At the time, Dan had assumed it was just part of his training. Thorn was preparing him for the Triune Hall trials—tests that would determine whether Dan was worthy of joining the elite ranks of warriors tasked with protecting the kingdom.

But now, looking back, Dan wondered if there had been more to it. Thorn had seemed distant, almost preoccupied, as if something weighed heavily on him. And then, the next day, he was gone.

Dan exhaled slowly, trying to quiet the storm of thoughts swirling in his mind. He couldn't shake the feeling that his parents knew more about Thorn's disappearance than they were letting on. Perhaps it was connected to whatever game they were playing with Alex.

He scanned the crowd once more, his eyes drawn again to the prince. Alex was laughing with a group of nobles, seemingly oblivious to the machinations surrounding him. For a moment, Dan considered crossing the room, approaching Alex, and warning him outright. Telling him everything—the pressure his parents were putting on him, the suspicion that Thorn's disappearance was part of something larger.

But he didn't move.

Even after all these years, the distance between them felt insurmountable. What could he say that wouldn't sound like an accusation? How could he make Alex understand that he didn't want any part of this—any part of the lies, the manipulation, the betrayal?

Dan's hand drifted once more to the hilt of his sword. He wished Thorn were here. Thorn would know what to do.

But Thorn wasn't here. And Dan was alone in a hall full of people, trapped between the weight of his family's expectations and the remnants of a broken friendship.

The music swelled, and the crowd shifted as new arrivals entered the hall, but Dan remained rooted to the spot, his mind racing. He didn't want to be here. He didn't want any part of this.

But he didn't know how to escape.

And somewhere in this vast hall, his sister Leandra moved among the crowds, no doubt weaving her own web of alliances and secrets. Dan felt a twinge of guilt; he should be by her side, protecting her, but the gulf between them seemed to widen with each passing day.

CHAPTER 2: WHISPERS IN THE GARDEN

LEANDRA TORREN STOOD NEAR the garden's edge, hidden by a curtain of ivy cascading over the stone wall. The evening air was cool against her skin, a welcome reprieve from the stuffy, perfume-filled halls of the gathering. She had slipped out for some fresh air, her patience with the endless gossip and shallow conversation long since worn thin. Her soft silk slippers barely made a sound as she moved along the shadowed edges of the terrace.

That was when she heard her father's voice, sharp and unmistakable, cutting through the night.

Leandra froze, her heart skipping a beat. She hadn't meant to overhear anything, but instinct told her to stay still. Lord Torren's voice, low and authoritative, carried a weight that made her stomach clench. Whatever he was discussing, it was not meant for casual ears. Carefully, she eased herself behind a stone column, letting the ivy hide her as she strained to listen.

"I don't care how it happens," her father was saying, his tone filled with his usual cold certainty. "Alex will go to the Red House. Once he's there, the scandal will take care of itself."

Leandra's blood ran cold. The Red House? She knew exactly what that meant. The Red Houses were illegal brothels, known for their excesses and depravity, frequented by those willing to risk ruin. If Alex—the crown prince—were caught in one of those places, it would destroy his reputation.

Her father's voice continued, calm and calculating. "Once the King realizes what his son has done, he'll be forced to come to us. We'll have the leverage we need to secure our position. Alex will be under our thumb, and the King will follow."

Leandra pressed herself further into the shadows, her pulse racing. Blackmail. Her father wasn't just plotting to humiliate Prince Alex—he was aiming to manipulate the King himself. The stakes were higher than anything she had imagined.

A second voice, deeper and unfamiliar, joined the conversation. "Are you sure Alex will fall for it?"

"He doesn't have to fall for anything," Lord Torren replied. "His so-called friends will lead him right to it. He'll be drunk, distracted, and once he's inside the Red House, the rest will be easy."

Leandra's heart pounded in her chest. This wasn't just a trap—they were pushing Alex into a disaster. And once he fell, her father would tighten his grip on the kingdom through blackmail.

Her thoughts immediately shifted to Dan. Was he part of this? Their father had paraded him around the gathering earlier, introducing him to important nobles, flaunting him as the perfect son. But Leandra wasn't sure how close their father kept Dan these days. Since their mother had taken such control over Leandra's time, forcing her to attend endless meetings, lessons, and tedious social events, she had barely seen her brother. Their father had always been more focused on Dan, while their mother preferred to shape Leandra to her own needs, keeping her busy with tasks and appearances that seemed meaningless.

For all Leandra knew, Dan might be as much in the dark as she was. Or perhaps he was deeply involved in their father's schemes, caught up in the political machinations their family was known for. It gnawed at her, this uncertainty about her brother's loyalties. How well did she even know him anymore? They had once been close, sharing secrets and finding solace in each other amid the pressures of their upbringing. But now, with so much distance—literal and emotional—she wasn't sure where Dan stood.

The memory of seeing him earlier in the night flashed in her mind. He had looked uncomfortable, stiff under the weight of their parents' expectations. He hadn't seemed like someone in on a plot, but Leandra had learned that in this world, appearances could be deceiving. She wanted to trust him, but their mother had worked hard to keep them separated, perhaps deliberately, as if ensuring they couldn't support each other against their parents' manipulation.

The voices of her father and his ally continued, but Leandra wasn't listening anymore. The weight of what she had overheard was enough. She had to do something. If she said nothing, Alex's downfall was guaranteed, and the consequences could ripple far beyond just him. But if she acted... she would be betraying her family. Or at least, her father.

But what loyalty did she owe them?

The thought burned in her mind, and she clenched her fists, feeling the familiar frustration rise within her. Lord Torren and Lady Torren had always used her and Dan as pawns in their endless pursuit of power. Her father, with his ruthless ambition, saw Dan as a means to cement their influence, while her mother had molded her into the perfect political tool. They had manipulated them both, keeping them apart, ensuring that neither of them had the freedom to make their own choices.

Leandra exhaled slowly, trying to quiet the storm in her thoughts. Dan deserved to know. Even if she wasn't sure where his loyalties lay, she couldn't keep this from him. He might be part of their father's plans, or he might not—but he deserved the chance to make his own decision. And if she approached him carefully, casually, as if she had overheard this by accident, he wouldn't suspect she had an agenda of her own.

The idea took root in her mind. She could warn Dan, plant the seed of doubt in his mind about their father's intentions. Maybe he would act. Or maybe, together, they could find a way to stop this.

She hesitated for a moment, considering her next move. It would be risky. If her father found out she had overheard this conversation, or worse, if he learned she had told Dan, there would be consequences. But Leandra was no longer willing to play their games, not without knowing the full stakes.

She cast one last glance into the shadows where her father's voice had faded, her resolve hardening. As she turned back towards the gathering, she caught sight of a Sword Guard's silver and gray uniform glinting in the moonlight, and a Shepherd's green robes disappearing around a corner. The members of the Triune Halls moved through the crowd with purpose, their alert gazes suggesting they sensed the undercurrents of danger swirling beneath the surface of the celebration.

Leandra's eyes swept over the opulent nobles, their wealth on display in gleaming jewels and fine silks, a stark contrast to the understated dignity of the Lawgivers in their navy and gold. And there, at the center of it all, stood the King and Alex, seemingly oblivious to the machinations surrounding them.

She would act. But she would do it carefully, in a way that would give her and Dan the chance to break free of their parents' control. And perhaps, in doing so, she might just save the fragile balance of power that held their kingdom together.

Chapter 3: Fractured Friendship

Prince Alex stood in the midst of the grand hall, the laughter and chatter of young nobles swirling around him, but his thoughts were far away. He wore the mask of royalty well—straight-backed, composed, his dark eyes betraying none of the unease he felt. As he nodded politely at some joke he hadn't really heard, he couldn't help but feel a gnawing emptiness beneath the surface.

His gaze swept across the room, taking in the diverse gathering. Sword Guards in their distinctive silver, black, and gray uniforms stood at strategic points, their vigilant eyes constantly scanning the crowd. Shepherds in their green and brown robes moved among the guests, offering quiet words of wisdom or comfort. Near the center of the room, a group of Lawgivers in their navy blue and gold attire—a less ornate echo of Alex's own royal garments—engaged in serious discussion.

Dan was here somewhere. He'd seen him earlier, standing stiffly beside his parents, his face a mask of polite indifference. But there had been no greeting between them, not even a shared glance. It was as if they were strangers, though it hadn't always been that way.

Alex swallowed hard, forcing a smile as another noble approached to exchange pleasantries. His mind drifted back, back to simpler days—before the weight of royal expectations had settled so heavily on his shoulders. He remembered the afternoons spent with Dan, the two of them racing through the gardens of the palace, challenging each other to sword fights with sticks, and talking about the grand adventures they'd have once they were older.

Dan had been his closest friend, once. Closer than any of the other noble children who orbited around him now, hoping for favors or alliances. With Dan, there had never been any pretenses, no expectations beyond what they'd built together as boys. Alex could almost hear Dan's laughter, clear and bright, from years ago—a sound that now seemed like it belonged to another lifetime.

He couldn't pinpoint the exact moment things had changed, but his twelfth birthday came to mind. It had been a grand affair, of course—his father had spared no expense to show the court that the young prince was growing into his role. Hundreds of guests, lavish decorations, a feast that seemed to stretch on forever. Dan had been there, standing among the nobles, but something had shifted that day.

Alex had noticed it in the way Dan's smile didn't quite reach his eyes, the way he seemed to linger on the edges of the celebration, no longer at his side like he used to be. At first, Alex had told himself it was nothing—that Dan was just tired, overwhelmed by the crowd. But as the years went by, the distance between them had grown.

Alex hadn't understood it then. He still didn't. Maybe it was just the natural drift that came with growing up.

What happened to us? Alex wondered as he scanned the room, his eyes lingering on where he'd last seen Dan. They were older now, and the world around them was more complicated than it had been when they were boys. Alex had his duties as prince, the constant weight of expectations pressing down on him. Every move he made was watched, every word scrutinized. The people here didn't care about who he really was—they cared about the power he represented, the alliances they could make, the favors they could win.

It was exhausting, pretending to be the prince everyone expected him to be.

And yet, he couldn't help but feel a pang of regret when he thought about Dan. They had been friends once—real friends. The kind of friends who could speak openly, who didn't care about titles or politics. Alex missed that. He missed him. But it seemed like that part of his life had slipped away, buried beneath years of royal obligations and whatever had pulled Dan in a different direction.

Alex shook himself, realizing he'd been standing in silence for too long. The young nobleman in front of him was still talking, oblivious to the prince's distraction, but Alex forced himself to focus.

"Forgive me," Alex said, his voice steady and polite. "I was lost in thought for a moment."

The noble smiled, eager to please. "No need, Your Highness. We all have much on our minds tonight."

Alex nodded absently, though his mind had already drifted again, back to Dan. There was a tension now, between them—one he couldn't fully explain but could always feel whenever they were in the same room. Alex wasn't sure if it was something his father had done, or Dan's, or if it was just the inevitable result of their different lives. But whatever it was, it hurt.

As he gazed around the room, Alex caught sight of a Shepherd speaking quietly with a group of nobles. The calm presence of the green-robed figure seemed to ease the tension in the air, if only for a moment. Nearby, a Sword Guard shifted position, silver and gray uniform gleaming in the light of the chandeliers. These members of the Triune Halls, Alex realized, were as much a part of the intricate dance of power as the nobles themselves.

But he knew the truth. It was too late now. They weren't boys any-more, and the roles they were forced to play—prince and noble—made it impossible to go back to the way things had been. Still, the longing for that lost friendship gnawed at him, especially on nights like this, when the weight of the crown felt unbearably heavy.

He stole another glance around the room, hoping to catch sight of Dan, if only for a moment. But even as his eyes searched the crowd, past the mingling nobles and the ever-watchful members of the Triune Halls, Alex knew that whatever they'd once had was gone, perhaps forever. And the ache of that loss was something no amount of royal training could ever teach him to forget.

Chapter 4: Tangled Webs

Leandra lingered by the marble balcony, eyes scanning the sea of young nobles milling about in their finest clothes, lost in chatter and laughter. The evening was in full swing, and yet she felt utterly alone in the crowd. Her thoughts churned restlessly, replaying her father's chilling words about the plot to ensnare Prince Alex.

Her father and the noble's scheme had rattled her more than she cared to admit. If their plan worked, Alex's reputation would be in tatters, and their father would gain the leverage he needed to manipulate the King. The consequences would be disastrous for the realm, but more immediately, it was a stark reminder of how deeply her parents used others—Dan, Alex, and even herself—as mere tools in their political games.

She hated it. All of it.

But what could she do?

Her hand tightened around the railing as her gaze swept across the grand hall, her thoughts drifting toward the Sword Guard Theran. Tall, handsome, and fiercely loyal to the King, Theran had caught her eye the moment she'd seen him. Unlike the conniving nobles who surrounded her, Theran exuded a quiet strength and an unshakable sense of honor. He seemed like the kind of man who could stand up to her father, who wouldn't be swept into the tide of blackmail and manipulation.

For a fleeting moment, she considered seeking him out. He could help her. He would listen. If anyone could put an end to her father's plot without implicating her directly, it would be Theran. The image of him flashed in her mind—his steady gaze, his hand resting on the hilt of his sword, ready to protect the King at any cost.

But what would he think of her? she thought bitterly. The daughter of Lord and Lady Torren, spilling family secrets to a Sword Guard.

Leandra shook her head. No, Theran was too risky. He was loyal to the King above all else, and if she went to him with this, there was no telling what the fallout would be. Her father would know it had come from her. Worse still, if it went wrong, she would lose what little freedom she had left. Her parents were already suffocating her—under their constant watch, molding her into the perfect pawn for their ambitions. If they knew she had turned on them, they would never let her out of their sight again.

She needed to be smarter about this. She couldn't act on impulse, no matter how tempting it was to trust Theran's honor. She had to tread carefully.

Her eyes drifted to another familiar figure in the crowd: Dan. He stood across the room, his expression tight, his posture rigid. He didn't belong here, and they both knew it. Their father had paraded him around earlier, showing him off to the other nobles like a prized possession. But she wasn't sure if their father was keeping Dan close or merely using him for appearances.

She'd barely seen Dan in the past months, their mother keeping her too busy with endless obligations, separating them so thoroughly that Leandra felt more like a stranger to him than a sister. The distance pained her. They had once been so close, and now it felt like they were both trapped in their own prisons, unable to help each other.

But maybe he could help her.

Dan wasn't in on their father's schemes; she was almost certain of that. He hated these kinds of events, despised the politics of their world even more than she did. But she also knew that their father had ways of twisting people to his will. Dan might already be tangled in his plans, without even knowing it.

Leandra exhaled slowly, resolving to try. If she could just nudge him, drop a few hints, maybe Dan would do the right thing. Maybe they could still salvage something from the wreckage their parents had made of their lives.

With measured steps, she made her way across the hall, slipping through the crowd unnoticed. Dan stood near the far end of the room, half-listening to some lord's monologue about trade routes, his eyes distant.

"Dan," she called softly when she reached him.

He turned, his brow furrowing in surprise. "Leandra. I didn't think you'd find time to come over here."

She forced a smile. "You know how Mother is," she replied lightly. "Always has me running from one conversation to another. But I needed a break, and… well, I thought I'd check on my brother."

His expression softened slightly, though the tension remained. "I suppose you've heard how Father's been dragging me around all night."

Leandra hesitated, glancing around to make sure no one was close enough to overhear. "I overheard something else, too," she said in a low voice, careful to maintain a casual tone. "Something about Alex. There's… talk of him being taken to a Red House."

Dan's eyes sharpened instantly, his posture stiffening. "What?"

Leandra shrugged, as though she didn't fully understand the gravity of her own words. "I'm not sure what's going on, but Father was speaking with someone about it. They seemed to think if Alex was caught there, it would… well, it wouldn't look good for him."

Dan's jaw tightened, and for a moment, she saw the flicker of conflict in his eyes. He cares, she thought, feeling a brief surge of hope. He might act on this.

"Why are you telling me this?" he asked, his voice low and cautious.

Leandra's heart thudded in her chest. She had to be careful. If she gave away too much, if she seemed too eager, he'd grow suspicious. "I thought you should know," she said simply, her voice soft but steady. "I'm not sure what Father's plans are, but… you were close with Alex once. Maybe you can help."

Dan stared at her for a long moment, his expression unreadable. Then, with a curt nod, he said, "Thanks for telling me, Leandra. I'll handle it."

She nodded, relief and anxiety warring in her chest. It was done. She had told him enough to act, without giving too much away. Now, it was up to Dan to do something about it.

As she turned to leave, her thoughts swirled with possibilities. What would happen if Dan got involved? What would Father do if he found out she had tipped him off? And what would happen if Alex was caught in this trap?

Leandra's mind raced, but one thought stood out above the rest: I need a plan. A way out. She couldn't stay in the grasp of her parents forever. Sooner or later, she would have to break free—find a way to live her own life, not the one they were forcing upon her.

Perhaps, after all of this, she could start to find that way. But for now, she had planted the seed. She just had to hope that Dan would see the truth and act before it was too late.

Chapter 5: Torn Loyalties

Dan stood by one of the ornate pillars in the grand hall, his mind racing as Leandra's words echoed in his head. They're planning to take Alex to a Red House. The thought of it churned in his gut. He glanced across the room to where Alex stood, surrounded by eager nobles, laughing and seemingly unaware of the storm brewing around him.

What should he do?

He clenched his jaw, feeling the weight of his father's expectations pressing down on him. Lord Torren had made his intentions clear earlier: Keep an eye on Alex. Listen for anything we can use. Dan hated the idea of spying on anyone, let alone someone who used to be his closest friend. But the image of Alex being dragged into a scandal—one that could ruin his future and strengthen their father's grip on the King—was too much to ignore.

Dan's eyes swept across the crowded hall, taking in the intricate dance of power and politics playing out before him. Nobles in their finest silks mingled with members of the Triune Halls, their conversations a mix of laughter and hushed whispers. He noticed a group of Lawgivers, their navy and gold attire marking them as the guardians of Septily's complex legal system, engaged in what looked like a heated debate near one of the windows.

His gaze drifted to a Shepherd standing quietly near a group of younger nobles. The green-robed figure's calm presence seemed to ease the tension around them, and for a moment, Dan considered approaching. Shepherds were known for their wisdom and discretion. Perhaps he could share his concerns without revealing too much, seek guidance on what to do.

But as he watched, he saw his father deep in conversation with one of the senior Shepherds. Lord Torren's face was a mask of respectful attention, but Dan knew that look. His father was fishing for information, weaving his web of influence.

Dan's fingers tightened into fists. If this went wrong, it wouldn't just be Alex who was hurt. Dan's family would use the fallout to gain more power, regardless of who got trampled in the process. His stomach twisted at the thought. Leandra's hint had been just vague enough to protect herself but clear enough to make Dan realize the gravity of the situation.

He had to do something.

But what? He couldn't go straight to Alex. The tension between them was too thick now, layered with years of unspoken grievances and the distance their families had forced between them. Alex wouldn't trust him, not after all this time. Dan could hardly blame him for that.

His eyes darted around the room again, this time landing on a group of Sword Guards near the main entrance. Their silver, black, and gray uniforms stood out against the colorful attire of the nobles. Dan's heart quickened as he recognized one of them—Zara. She wasn't just any guard; she was one of the few people Dan had learned to trust since his training began with Thorn, who had been friends with her. Zara had always been straightforward with him, treating him not as a noble's son but as someone who might someday earn her respect. She had been part of Alex's personal guard for months, and if anyone could keep an eye on him, it would be her.

Dan took a breath and started toward her, weaving through the crowd. As he neared, Zara's sharp green eyes flicked in his direction, recognizing him instantly. She gave a small nod but didn't move from her post by the door, her hand resting lightly on the hilt of her sword.

"Zara," Dan greeted her, his voice low. He could feel his heart pounding in his chest as he came to stand beside her, keeping his tone casual. "I need to talk to you. Privately."

She raised an eyebrow but didn't speak immediately. Instead, she glanced over his shoulder, scanning the room for any unwelcome ears. Once satisfied, she nodded curtly and led him toward a quieter corner of the hall, where the hum of conversation was more distant.

"What's this about?" Zara asked, her voice low but firm.

Dan hesitated, unsure how much he could say. He trusted Zara, but if this got out too soon, it could backfire. He didn't want to see Alex caught in a scandal—especially not because of something he had done. But Leandra's warning was clear enough that ignoring it was no longer an option.

"I overheard something," Dan said, keeping his voice measured. "There's a plot… involving Alex. They're planning to lead him somewhere tonight. Somewhere dangerous."

Zara's eyes narrowed. "Dangerous how?"

Dan shifted uncomfortably, choosing his words carefully. "It involves a Red House. If he's seen there… well, you know what that would mean for him. And for the King."

Zara's expression hardened. She knew exactly what Dan was implying. A scandal involving Alex and an illegal establishment like that could be enough to wreck the prince's reputation. The King would be forced to act, and Alex's enemies would pounce on the opportunity to bring him down.

"Who's behind it?" she asked quietly.

Dan shook his head. "I can't say for certain. But it's happening tonight. I'm sure of it."

Zara's gaze remained fixed on him for a moment longer before she exhaled softly. "You're doing the right thing, Dan. But this is going to get messy if Alex sneaks off without us knowing."

Dan winced. "That's what I'm worried about. I need you to keep an eye on him, make sure he doesn't slip away. He's... not himself lately. There's too much at stake for him to be caught up in this."

Zara nodded, her expression serious. "I'll handle it. Don't worry, he won't go anywhere without us watching him."

Dan felt a brief surge of relief, but it was quickly drowned out by the knot of anxiety in his chest. He knew Zara would do her best to prevent Alex from walking into the trap, but the risk was still there. Alex was stubborn, and if he wanted to sneak off, no amount of Sword Guards would stop him.

"Thanks, Zara," he said quietly. "I don't know what my father's up to, but I'm sure he'll be watching too."

Zara's eyes darkened. "Be careful, Dan. There's more than one way to get caught up in all of this."

Dan nodded, the weight of her words sinking in. He turned to leave, but before he did, Zara's voice stopped him.

"Dan," she said softly. "I know it's hard... balancing loyalty to your family with what's right. But don't lose sight of who you are in all of this."

Her words struck deeper than she probably intended. Dan swallowed hard, giving her a brief nod before heading back into the crowd. Who I am, he thought bitterly. It was hard to know anymore. Torn between his father's demands and his own conscience, he felt like a blade caught between a whetstone and a hammer, reshaped by forces he couldn't fully control.

As he glanced at Alex from across the room, still laughing with his circle of admirers, Dan felt the old ache of friendship stir within him. He didn't want to see Alex fall, even if their friendship had frayed beyond recognition.

He had to stop this, No matter what it cost him, he wouldn't let Alex get pulled into the abyss.

Chapter 6: A Prince's Folly

Prince Alex leaned against the banquet table, his goblet of wine swirling with an alluring crimson hue. The lively laughter and chatter of the gathering around him felt distant, like echoes reverberating through a hollow chamber. He watched the nobles mingle, their faces bright with mirth, while he remained an outsider, cocooned in an unsettling loneliness that gripped him like a vice.

From across the room, he caught sight of his father, King Xandros, deep in conversation with a group of Lawgivers, their navy and gold attire a somber contrast to the colorful nobles. The King's face was stern, focused on matters of state even in the midst of celebration. Alex felt a pang of longing for his father's attention, a feeling he'd grown accustomed to over the years.

His gaze drifted to a nearby Shepherd, offering words of wisdom to a cluster of young nobles. The green-robed figure's serene presence only highlighted Alex's inner turmoil. He knew his duty, understood the weight of the crown that would one day rest upon his brow. But standing here now, surrounded by the jovial façade, the empty weight of that duty settled heavily on his shoulders. It felt less like a privilege and more like a cage, confining him to a role he didn't fully understand.

"Your Highness," a familiar voice called out, cutting through his reverie. "You look like you could use some company."

Alex turned to see the Harnen brothers, Callum and Rowan, approaching with easy grins. The noble siblings had been his companions for years, often leading him into adventures that skirted the edge of propriety. Their presence was both a comfort and a source of anxiety—he knew they meant well, but their ideas of fun often led to trouble.

"Callum, Rowan," Alex greeted them, forcing a smile. "Enjoying the festivities?"

Callum, the elder of the two, laughed. "As much as one can enjoy such a stuffy affair. But we've got an idea to liven things up a bit."

Alex felt a flicker of wariness. "What did you have in mind?"

Rowan leaned in, his voice low and conspiratorial. "There's a gathering outside the castle walls. Something more... exciting than this dull party. What do you say we slip away for a bit of real fun?"

Before Alex could respond, he noticed his father making his way towards the exit, flanked by several Sword Guards. The King paused briefly, scanning the room until his eyes met Alex's. For a moment, Alex hoped his father might approach, might spare a word for his son. But King Xandros merely gave a curt nod before turning away, leaving the celebration behind.

The sting of dismissal was sharp, fueling the loneliness that had been Alex's constant companion. He turned back to the Blackwood brothers, who were watching him with a mixture of sympathy and mischief.

"Here," Callum said, pressing a fresh goblet into Alex's hand. "This'll help take the edge off."

Alex hesitated, a flicker of caution igniting in his mind. But the warmth of the goblet and the inviting aroma of the wine momentarily dulled his apprehensions. He took a sip, the rich taste comforting as it slid down his throat. Yet he couldn't shake the nagging sense that something was off.

"Your father," Rowan said, his tone carefully casual, "he still treats you like a child, doesn't he? Always too busy for his own son."

The words struck a chord, stirring a mix of frustration and yearning within Alex. His father's distant demeanor weighed heavily on him, as if he had yet to prove himself worthy of the crown.

"Perhaps it's time you showed him—showed everyone—that you're not just a boy anymore," Callum suggested, his eyes gleaming. "Come with us tonight. Prove you are a man in all the ways that matter."

Alex's heart raced, the camaraderie of the gathering shifting into something darker. As he caught sight of Dan and a Sword Guard—was that Zara?—leaning their heads together across the room, a pang of betrayal pierced through the growing fog in his mind. The friendship he had once shared with Dan felt like a distant memory, now tainted by the years of distance between them.

"Look at them," Rowan remarked, his voice low. "Seems your old friend has found a new ally in your Sword Guard. Perhaps they have plans that don't include you."

The insinuation stung. Alex felt his chest tighten, a mix of anger and sorrow boiling beneath the surface. Were they plotting something? The drink intensified his emotions, swirling his thoughts into a chaotic storm.

"I can do this," he muttered to himself, the urgency of the moment gripping him. He would prove them all wrong.

Callum grinned, sensing Alex's resolve weakening. "So, what do you say? Ready for a real adventure?"

Alex hesitated for a moment, his gaze sweeping across the hall one last time. He saw the Lawgivers in their serious discussions, the Shepherds offering guidance, the Sword Guards ever vigilant. This was his world, his duty. But tonight, it felt like a prison.

"Let's go," he said, his voice firmer than he felt. He could slip away, escape the suffocating confines of the castle and the expectations that loomed over him. He would seize this opportunity to prove himself, to break free from the bonds that held him captive.

As the Harnen brothers led him towards a side exit, the laughter of the party faded into a distant murmur. Alex glanced back one last time at Dan and Zara, their figures slowly blurring into the crowd. A mixture of betrayal and resolve surged within him, propelling him forward into the unknown.

Chapter 7: A Light in the Darkness

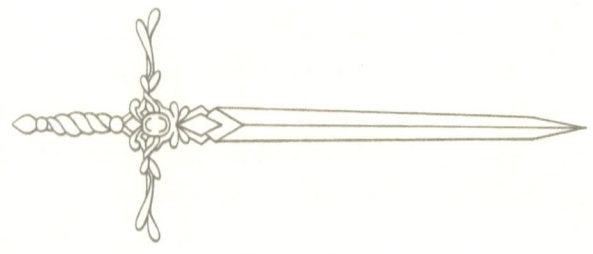

Farrald stood at the edge of the grand hall, his back pressed against the cool stone wall. The opulence of the Unity Gathering overwhelmed his senses—glittering chandeliers, flowing silks, and the constant hum of laughter and conversation. He tugged self-consciously at the sleeve of his best tunic, painfully aware of how plain it looked among the finery surrounding him.

"Lord of Light, guide my steps," he whispered, a prayer as familiar to him as breathing. The words brought a measure of comfort, even as he felt more out of place than ever before.

His eyes scanned the crowd, marveling at the diversity of the gathering. Nobles in their rich attire mingled freely, their jewels catching the light. Members of the Triune Halls moved with purpose through the throng—Sword Guards in their silver, black, and gray; Lawgivers in navy and gold; and Shepherds in their simple green or brown robes.

Farrald's heart ached at the sight of the Shepherds. That was where he belonged, he was sure of it. He could almost feel the weight of the silver pendant around his neck, could imagine himself offering words of comfort and guidance to those in need. But his father's words echoed in his mind, as unyielding as the desert rocks of home: "You have two choices, boy. The Watch Guard or the family business. That's it."

He sighed, his thoughts drifting to Juliay. He could almost hear her laugh, see the way her eyes crinkled at the corners when she smiled.

"You'll do what's right," she had told him before he left. "You always do." But what was right? Honor his family's wishes or follow the calling of his heart?

A flurry of movement near the center of the hall caught Farrald's attention. A young man, not much older than himself, stood surrounded by admirers. He was dressed more richly than anyone else in the room, his attire a masterpiece of deep blues and gold. There was something about him—an air of authority, perhaps—that made Farrald curious. But before he could ponder it further, his father's booming voice cut through his thoughts.

"There he is! Quinn, my good man, let me introduce you to my son, Farrald!"

Farrald felt his cheeks burn as his father approached, leading a tall, craggy-faced man in the silver, black, and gray uniform of the Watch Guard. His father's gaudy merchant's robes seemed even more out of place next to the guard's practical attire.

"Farrald, this is Quinn of the Watch Guard," his father announced, clapping a hand on Farrald's shoulder. "He's agreed to take you on for training. Quite an honor, isn't it? I was just telling Quinn here about our family's business connections. Did you know, Quinn, that we supply half the silk in the Desert District?"

Quinn's face remained impassive, his sharp eyes moving between Farrald and his father. He offered a slight nod but said nothing.

Farrald wished the floor would open up and swallow him whole. He could see that Quinn was not impressed by his father's showy manners or boasts about their merchant success.

"It's an honor to meet you, sir," Farrald managed, trying to keep his voice steady.

Quinn's gaze settled on Farrald, assessing. When he spoke, his voice was low and gravelly, each word carefully chosen. "The Watch Guard requires discipline and dedication. It's not an easy path."

Farrald swallowed hard. "I understand, sir. I'm prepared to work hard."

His father beamed, oblivious to the tension. "That's my boy! He'll do you proud, Quinn. Now, if you'll excuse me, I see the Silk Merchant's Guild representative over there. Must go say hello!"

As his father bustled away, Farrald felt a mix of relief and embarrassment. He glanced at Quinn, unsure what to say.

The older man's eyes had already shifted, scanning the room with quiet intensity. Farrald realized that Quinn was here not just as a representative of the Watch Guard, but as an observer, taking in every detail of the gathering.

After a moment of silence, Quinn spoke again, his voice still low. "Meet me at the East Gate courtyard at midnight. Your training begins tomorrow. You'll need to know what to bring."

Farrald's eyes widened in surprise. "Tonight? But I thought—"

Quinn's stern gaze silenced him. "Midnight. Don't be late." With that, he moved away, blending into the crowd with surprising ease for such an imposing figure.

Left alone once more, Farrald felt a mixture of excitement and anxiety wash over him. Tomorrow? He had thought he'd have more time to prepare, to say goodbye to the life he knew. But perhaps this was better—less time to second-guess himself, less time for doubt to creep in.

Here he was, a merchant's son from the Desert District, breathing the same air as the most powerful people in the kingdom. And tomorrow, he would begin a new life with the Watch Guard.

A commotion near the center of the hall caught Farrald's attention. A young man, dressed more richly than anyone else in deep blues and gold, was being led towards a side exit by two other nobles. There was something off about the scene—the young man's steps were unsteady, his eyes unfocused. The two nobles flanking him wore expressions that made Farrald uneasy, a mix of triumph and mischief that sent a chill down his spine.

Farrald frowned, his instincts telling him that something was amiss. The young man—who he now realized must be someone of great importance, perhaps even royalty—seemed to be in no condition to leave the gathering. Yet no one else appeared to be paying attention to their departure.

He glanced around, hoping to catch the eye of a Sword Guard or a Shepherd, someone who could intervene. But the crowd had shifted, obscuring his view of the exit where the young man had disappeared.

Farrald felt a surge of anxiety. Should he say something? Do something? He was just a merchant's son from the Desert District, far from home and out of his depth in this world of power and politics. But the teachings of the Lord of Light echoed in his mind: "To witness injustice and remain silent is to be complicit in its act."

With a deep breath, Farrald pushed himself away from the wall, determined to find someone who could help. As he weaved through the crowd, he caught sight of a familiar craggy face—Quinn, lurking at the edges of the crowd.

"Sir Quinn," Farrald called out, his voice barely audible above the din of the gathering. To his relief, Quinn turned, his sharp eyes focusing on Farrald with recognition.

"What is it, boy?" Quinn asked, his tone gruff but not unkind.

Farrald swallowed hard, suddenly aware of how his concerns might sound. "Sir, I... I saw something strange. A young man, dressed very finely, being led out of the hall. He didn't look well, and the men with him... something didn't feel right."

Quinn's expression sharpened, a flicker of alarm passing over his features. "Describe the young man," he demanded.

"Tall, blonde hair, dressed in deep blue and gold. He looked important," Farrald replied, the words tumbling out in a rush. "They went towards the eastern exit, I think."

Quinn cursed under his breath, his hand moving to the hilt of his sword. "You did well to tell me, boy. Now listen carefully. Go to the East Gate courtyard and wait there. Don't leave, no matter what you hear or see. Understand?"

Farrald nodded, a mixture of relief and trepidation washing over him. "Yes, sir. But what's happening? Is there something I can do to help?"

Quinn's stern gaze softened for a moment. "You've done your part. Now it's time for the Watch Guard to do ours. Remember, East Gate courtyard. Midnight. Don't be late."

With that, Quinn strode away, signaling to other Sword Guards as he moved. Farrald watched him go, his heart racing with the realization that he had stumbled upon something far bigger than he could have imagined.

Left alone once more, Farrald felt a mixture of pride and anxiety wash over him. He had done the right thing, he was sure of it. But what consequences would his actions have? And what dangers awaited the young man who had been led away?

"Guide my steps, Lord of Light," he whispered again, feeling the warmth of his faith wrap around him like a comforting embrace. "Show me the path I'm meant to walk."

As if in answer, a sense of calm settled over him. He might not know exactly where his journey would lead, but he knew he wouldn't walk it alone. With one last glance at the crowd, Farrald straightened his shoulders. He had a few hours left before his midnight meeting—hours that would no doubt be filled with uncertainty, quiet observation, and prayer. He would listen and learn.

Perhaps, watching the Shepherds would help him become better at being a Watch Guard.

Chapter 8: Shadows and Secrets

Dan's eyes narrowed as he caught sight of Alex being led away by the Harnen brothers. The prince's unsteady gait and unfocused gaze set off alarm bells in his mind. Something was very wrong.

"Zara," he hissed, grabbing the Sword Guard's attention. "Look."

Zara's hand instinctively moved to the hilt of her sword as she followed Dan's gaze. "Damn," she muttered. "They've drugged him."

"We need to follow them," Dan said, already moving.

Zara nodded briskly. "I'll alert Captain Oren. He's just over there. You stay on their tail. Be careful, and don't engage unless absolutely necessary."

Dan didn't wait to see Zara step away. He slipped through the crowd, keeping his eyes fixed on Alex and the Harnen brothers. They were moving with purpose, steering the stumbling prince towards a less populated area of the castle.

As Dan rounded a corner, he caught a glimpse of the trio ducking into what looked like a plain stone wall. His heart raced. A secret passage? He'd heard rumors of hidden routes throughout the castle, but he'd never seen one himself.

Approaching cautiously, Dan ran his hands over the stone where they'd disappeared. After a moment, he felt a slight give in one of the blocks. He pressed, and a section of the wall swung inward silently.

Taking a deep breath, Dan plunged into the darkness beyond. The passage was narrow and damp, lit sporadically by sputtering torches. He could hear echoing footsteps and muffled voices ahead. Moving as quietly as he could, Dan followed the sounds, his mind racing with questions and fears.

The tunnel seemed to slope downward, twisting and turning. Dan lost all sense of direction, but he pressed on, driven by concern for Alex. After what felt like an eternity, he saw a faint glimmer of moonlight ahead.

Slowing his pace, Dan approached the exit cautiously. He emerged into a small, overgrown courtyard. The castle walls loomed above, but he realized with a start that he was now outside the gates. The secret passage had led them beyond the castle's defenses.

In the distance, he could see the Harnen brothers supporting Alex between them, making their way down a narrow street. Dan followed, keeping to the shadows, his heart pounding in his chest.

As they turned a corner, Dan's blood ran cold. A red lamp hung outside an ornate gate, casting an eerie glow on the cobblestones. The Red House. He'd heard whispers of such places—noble houses turned into exclusive brothels for a night, catering to the most depraved desires of the wealthy and powerful.

Dan hesitated at the corner, conflicted. He couldn't go in there. The risk of being seen, of being implicated in whatever scandal was about to unfold, was too great. But could he leave Alex alone? His oldest friend, despite the years of distance between them?

"No, Alex," Dan whispered, watching as the Harnen brothers led the prince through the gate, disappearing into the shadowy courtyard beyond.

Should he go back? Try to find his way through the tunnel to alert Zara? But what if something happened to Alex in the meantime?

As Dan stood there, torn between duty and friendship, a hand clasped his shoulder. He spun around, startled, to find himself face to face with a grizzled man wearing the silver, black, and gray uniform of the Watch

Guard. Dan's heart raced, recognizing the elite force known for their fierce combat skills and reputation as silent observers.

"Easy, lad," the man said, his voice low and gravelly. "I'm Quinn of the Watch Guard. You've been following the prince, haven't you?"

Dan nodded, a mixture of relief and apprehension washing over him. "Yes, sir. They've taken him into the Red House. He's been drugged, I think. I wasn't sure what to do—"

Quinn's expression hardened, his eyes scanning the area with practiced efficiency. "You did right by following them. I need to alert my team. We'll handle this carefully."

"I want to help," Dan said, his voice firm despite the tremor in his hands. "I can't just leave Alex in there."

Quinn studied him for a moment, his weathered face unreadable. Then, to Dan's surprise, he gave a curt nod. "Alright, lad. But you stay put right here. Don't move, don't try to enter. Understand?"

"Yes, sir," Dan agreed, both relieved and anxious to be included.

"I'll be back with reinforcements. We'll get him out together," Quinn assured him, then melted into the shadows with a swiftness that spoke of years of training.

Left alone, Dan pressed himself against the cool stone of a nearby building, his eyes fixed on the red lamp that marked the entrance to the brothel. The wait was excruciating. Every moment felt like an eternity, each sound from within the building sending a jolt of fear through him. What was happening to Alex? Were the Harnen brothers carrying out their plan even now?

Minutes ticked by, though it felt much longer to Dan. The night air grew colder, and he found himself shivering, though whether from the chill or from nerves, he couldn't tell. He strained his ears for any sign of Quinn's return, but the street remained quiet save for the occasional burst of laughter from within.

Doubt began to creep in. Had Quinn truly accepted his help, or had the seasoned and mysterious Watch Guard simply been placating him? Should he have insisted on going with Quinn? Or worse, had something gone wrong? The possibilities tormented Dan as he stood in the shadows, feeling helpless and increasingly afraid.

He thought of Alex, of the friendship they once shared. The laughter, the dreams, the promises of loyalty that seemed so easy to make as children. How had they drifted so far apart? And now, with Alex in danger, would Dan even get the chance to make things right?

The continued sounds of merriment from the Red House made Dan's stomach churn. His hand instinctively went to the hilt of his sword. Every instinct screamed at him to rush in, to find Alex and drag him out of there. But the Watch Guard's orders held him back. He had to trust that they knew what they were doing, that their reputation for efficiency and discretion was well-earned.

Still, as the minutes ticked by with no sign of Quinn or his reinforcements, Dan's resolve began to waver. How long was too long to wait? At what point did loyalty to a friend outweigh following the orders of a stranger, even one from the legendary Watch Guard?

The red lamp flickered, casting dancing shadows on the cobblestones. Dan's eyes never left the ornate gate, willing it to open, to reveal Alex safe and sound, or Quinn returning with help. But the gate remained closed, an impassable barrier between Dan and his friend.

As he stood there, the weight of the night pressing down on him, Dan realized that this moment of waiting might be the true test of his character. Not the flash of heroic action, but the patience to do what was right, even when every fiber of his being urged him to act.

But patience had its limits. And as another peal of laughter echoed from the Red House, something inside Dan snapped. He couldn't wait any longer. Watch Guard or no Watch Guard, he had to do something.

His heart pounding, Dan took a step towards the ornate gate. Then another. His hand tightened on the hilt of his sword as he approached the entrance to the Red House. Whatever lay beyond that gate, whatever dangers awaited, Dan knew one thing for certain: he was done waiting.

With a deep breath, he reached for the gate, ready to face whatever consequences lay ahead. Alex needed him, and this time, Dan wouldn't let his friend down.

Chapter 9: Whispers and Shadows

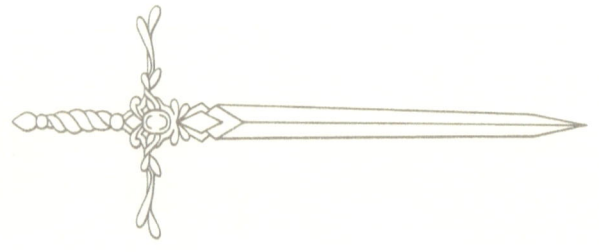

Leandra stood at the edge of the grand hall, her eyes scanning the crowd with growing unease. The Unity Gathering continued in full swing around her, but her mind was far from the festivities. She had watched Alex leave, his steps unsteady and his eyes unfocused, led away by those troublesome Harnen brothers. Then Dan had slipped out after them, his face a mask of concern. And now Zara, the Sword Guard, was urgently speaking with her superiors.

Something was very wrong.

Leandra's heart raced as she considered her options. Who could she talk to? Who would listen without immediately reporting back to her parents? Her gaze drifted across the room, searching for a friendly face or a potential ally.

That's when she saw him again. Theran. He was walking towards one of the side exits, deep in conversation with Shepherd Jordan. Leandra felt a familiar flutter in her chest as she watched Theran, admiring the way he carried himself with quiet confidence. For a moment, she was tempted to follow, to find an excuse to join their conversation. But she hesitated, knowing that her infatuation was just that – a schoolgirl crush on someone she barely knew.

As Theran and the Shepherd disappeared from view, Leandra's anxiety returned full force. She needed to do something, to tell someone about the danger Alex might be in. But who?

"Leandra!" Her mother's sharp voice cut through her thoughts like a knife. "Where is your brother?"

Leandra turned to face Lady Torren, whose eyes were narrowed with suspicion and barely contained anger. For a moment, Leandra considered telling the truth, but the words stuck in her throat. Instead, she found herself lying.

"I'm not sure, Mother," she said, keeping her voice steady. "Perhaps he stepped out for some air? I was actually feeling a bit tired myself. I was thinking of retiring for the evening."

Her mother's expression hardened. "Tired? Don't be ridiculous. You have a duty here, Leandra. I expect you to mingle, to listen, to gather information. That's your role, and I won't have you neglecting it because you're 'tired.'"

The harshness in her mother's tone made Leandra flinch. "Yes, Mother. I'm sorry. I'll get back to it right away."

Lady Torren leaned in close, her voice a threatening whisper. "See that you do. And find your brother. I won't have either of you embarrassing this family tonight. Am I clear?"

"Crystal clear, Mother," Leandra replied, her throat tight.

As her mother swept away to rejoin a group of nobles, Leandra felt a wave of despair wash over her. She couldn't bear the thought of more small talk, more vapid conversations thinly veiling attempts at political maneuvering. Instead, she found herself moving towards the balcony, seeking a moment of solitude.

The cool night air was a relief as she stepped outside. Leandra moved to the far corner of the balcony, hidden from view by a large potted plant. Here, alone in the shadows, she finally let her composed facade crumble.

Tears pricked at her eyes as she gazed out over the city. She felt trapped, caught in a web of expectations and manipulation. Her parents saw her as nothing more than a tool, a means to gather intelligence and further their ambitions. And Dan... where was he now? What danger had he walked into, trying to help Alex?

For a wild moment, Leandra considered leaving it all behind. She could run away, join the Triune Halls perhaps. But even as the thought crossed her mind, she dismissed it with a bitter laugh. What skills did she have that would be of use to the Sword Guards, Shepherds, or Lawgivers?

Then, unbidden, a memory surfaced. The weight of a practice sword in her hand, the patient instructions of Sword Guard Thorn guiding her movements. Those secret lessons, stolen moments away from her parents' watchful eyes, had been a rare taste of freedom. Thorn had seen potential in her, had taught her more than just swordplay. He had shown her what it meant to have honor, to serve a purpose greater than oneself.

Leandra's heart ached with a fresh wave of longing. Thorn's disappearance had left a void in her life, another loss in a world that seemed determined to isolate her. She wasn't skilled enough to join the Sword Guards, not yet. But Thorn had believed in her, had seen something in her that went beyond her family name or her role as a noble's daughter.

As she stood there, looking out over the city, a new resolve began to form in Leandra's mind. She might be trapped for now, but she wouldn't be forever. She had skills her parents didn't know about, a strength they couldn't see. And she had a mission now, two-fold and crystal clear.

First, she would do whatever it took to protect Alex and Dan. They were out there somewhere, possibly in danger, and she wouldn't stand idly by while her brother and the prince faced unknown threats.

But beyond that immediate concern, a new determination took root. She would find Thorn. His disappearance had never sat right with her, and now, with everything else going on, she couldn't shake the feeling that it was all connected somehow. Thorn wouldn't have abandoned them without reason. If he was out there, she would find him. And maybe, in doing so, she would find her own path as well.

Leandra took a deep breath, feeling a sense of purpose settle over her. She couldn't afford to be seen as vulnerable or emotional, but she could use the skills she had - both those taught by her parents and those learned in secret with Thorn - to start unraveling the mysteries surrounding her.

With one last glance at the city below, Leandra straightened her shoulders and turned back towards the grand hall. The night was far from over, and she had work to do. She would play the part her mother demanded, for now. But behind the facade of the perfect noble daughter, Leandra's mind would be working, planning, gathering every scrap of information she could.

For Alex, for Dan, for Thorn, and for herself, Leandra would become the force her parents never imagined she could be. The thought brought a small, determined smile to her lips as she stepped back into the light of the grand hall, ready to do her work.

CHAPTER 10: A PRINCE'S TEMPTATION

THE WORLD SWAM IN and out of focus as Alex leaned against the wall of the Red House's entry hall. The Harnen brothers' voices seemed to come from far away, their laughter grating on his nerves. He blinked, trying to clear the fog from his mind, but the drug they'd given him still held its grip.

Scantily clad women moved about the room, their figures blurring in Alex's vision. He felt a mixture of fascination and discomfort, unable to reconcile their willingness to engage in such activities with his own upbringing. A part of him was curious, tempted even, but a stronger part recoiled at the wrongness of it all.

"Come on, Your Highness," Callum Harnen's voice cut through the haze. "Pick one and become a real man. It's about time, isn't it?"

Alex shook his head, instantly regretting the motion as the room spun. "I... I don't think..."

"Don't think, that's the point," Rowan chimed in, his words slurring slightly. "Feel. Experience. Live a little!"

A woman with long, dark hair approached Alex, her hand reaching out to caress his cheek. He flinched away, his back pressing harder against the wall. "I... I'm fine here," he mumbled, heat rising to his face.

The woman pouted but moved away, only to be replaced by another. And another. Each touch, each whispered invitation sent conflicting waves of desire and shame through Alex. His body responded traitorously, even as his mind screamed that this was wrong.

Time seemed to lose all meaning. Alex remained rooted to his spot, neither accepting nor fully rejecting the advances. The Harnen brothers' taunts became background noise, drowned out by the war in Alex's own mind.

As the fog in his head began to clear, the reality of his situation started to sink in. What was he doing here? What would his father say if he knew? The thought of disappointing the king, of bringing shame to the crown, made Alex's stomach churn.

Suddenly, the door burst open. Alex blinked in surprise as a familiar figure strode in, face set in grim determination.

"Dan?" Alex's voice was barely a whisper.

Before he could process what was happening, Dan had crossed the room and yanked Alex to his feet. "We're leaving. Now."

"Hey!" Callum protested, stumbling to his feet. "You can't just—"

"Watch me," Dan growled, already dragging Alex towards the door.

The cool night air hit Alex like a slap to the face as they emerged from the Red House. He stumbled, nearly falling, but Dan's grip on his arm kept him upright.

"What do you think you're doing?" Alex demanded, anger rising to replace his earlier shame and confusion. "You can't just barge in and—"

"Saving you from making the biggest mistake of your life," Dan cut him off. "Or didn't you realize the trouble you'd be in if you were caught in there?"

Alex's face burned with a mixture of anger and embarrassment. "I didn't ask for your help! I had everything under control!"

Dan snorted. "Really? Because from where I was standing, it looked like you were about five minutes away from—"

"Shut up!" Alex shouted, wrenching his arm from Dan's grasp. "You have no right to judge me. You're not my friend anymore, remember? You're just another noble trying to curry favor with my father!"

Hurt flashed across Dan's face, quickly replaced by frustration. "Is that what you think? I'm trying to help you, Alex!"

"Help me?" Alex scoffed. "More like help yourself. I bet you can't wait to run to my father and tell him all about how you 'saved' the prince. Well, I don't need your help or your false friendship!"

Before Dan could retort, the sound of approaching footsteps caught their attention. Alex's blood ran cold as he recognized the uniforms of the approaching Sword Guards.

Panic and anger surged through him in equal measure. This was it. He was caught. His father would hear about this, and all because Dan couldn't mind his own business.

"This is your fault," Alex hissed at Dan, his voice low and venomous. "If you had just left me alone..."

The Sword Guards were getting closer now. Alex straightened his posture, trying to gather whatever dignity he had left. He might be in trouble, but he was still the prince. And right now, that meant finding a way out.

As the first Sword Guard reached them, Alex pointed at Dan. "This man brought me here against my will," he lied, his voice steady despite the churning in his gut. "I want him arrested."

The look of betrayal on Dan's face almost made Alex falter. But it was too late now. The words were out, and Alex was committed to his course.

To Alex's surprise, however, the Sword Guards didn't immediately move to arrest Dan. Instead, they exchanged a glance before one of them spoke. "Your Highness, I'm afraid we'll need both of you to come with us. The situation requires... clarification."

"What?" Alex sputtered, indignation rising. "Do you know who I am? I gave you an order!"

"With all due respect, Your Highness," the guard replied, his tone firm but not unkind, "our orders come from higher up. Both of you will need to explain your presence here tonight."

As the guards moved to restrain both Alex and Dan, Alex felt a mixture of shock and fear. This wasn't how it was supposed to go. He was the prince; his word should have been enough.

In the midst of his rising panic, Alex caught a glimpse of movement in the shadows nearby. For a brief moment, he locked eyes with a grizzled man in the uniform of the Watch Guard. The man's piercing gaze seemed to see right through Alex, and a chill ran down his spine.

As quickly as he had appeared, the mysterious figure melted back into the darkness, leaving Alex to wonder if he had imagined it in his drug-addled state.

The night's temptations may have passed, but as the Sword Guards led both Alex and Dan away, the prince realized that the consequences were only beginning to unfold. And somewhere in the shadows, unseen eyes were watching it all unfold.

CHAPTER 11: TRUTH AND CONSEQUENCES

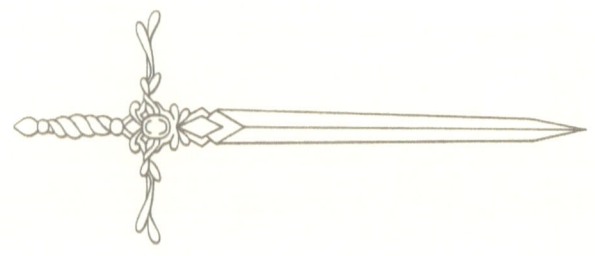

DAN'S HEART POUNDED IN his chest as he stood before King Xandros in the royal private office. The room, despite its opulence, felt suffocating. To his left, Alex stood rigid, his face a mask of barely contained anger and fear. A Lawgiver and a Shepherd stood silently to the side, their presence adding weight to the gravity of the situation.

King Xandros's eyes, sharp and piercing, moved between Dan and Alex. When he spoke, his voice was low and controlled, but laden with disappointment.

"The Red Hand," the King began, "is a blight on our world. Their influence corrupts, their actions destroy. And yet, my own son nearly fell into their trap." He fixed his gaze on Alex, who seemed to shrink under the scrutiny. "I expected better from you, Alex. I hoped you understood the responsibility that comes with your position."

Alex opened his mouth to speak, but a raised hand from his father silenced him.

"You will listen now," King Xandros said firmly. "Your actions tonight have not only endangered yourself but potentially the entire kingdom. I hope you understand the gravity of what could have happened."

Dan watched as Alex's shoulders slumped, the prince's earlier bravado crumbling under his father's words.

Then, the King's attention turned to Dan. "And you, young Torren. What exactly were you doing at the Red House?"

Dan swallowed hard, feeling the weight of the moment. This was his chance – perhaps his only chance – to do the right thing. He straightened his back and met the King's gaze.

"Your Majesty," he began, his voice steadier than he felt, "I followed Alex to protect him. I... I overheard plans. My father..." Dan hesitated, the words sticking in his throat. But he pushed on. "My father plotted to use Alex's indiscretion to blackmail you, Your Majesty. I couldn't let that happen."

A heavy silence fell over the room. Dan could feel Alex's eyes on him, but he didn't dare look. Instead, he kept his gaze fixed on the King, whose expression had turned thoughtful.

"I see," King Xandros said after a long moment. "And tell me, Dan Torren, do you believe you deserve a reward for your actions tonight?"

The question caught Dan off guard. He felt a flutter of fear in his stomach, unsure of how to respond. But as he considered the King's words, he knew what he had to say.

"Your Majesty," Dan said, his voice barely above a whisper, "if I may... I don't seek a reward. But I do have a request." He took a deep breath. "I wish to join the Watch Guard. To serve a more noble purpose than what my father has planned for me."

King Xandros's eyebrows raised slightly, a flicker of surprise crossing his face. He nodded slowly. "An interesting request. And one I'm inclined to grant." Then, his gaze shifted to Alex. "In fact, I believe my son will be joining you."

"What?" Alex exclaimed, breaking his silence. "Father, you can't be serious! I'm the prince, not some common—"

"Enough!" King Xandros's voice rang out, silencing Alex immediately. "You have demonstrated tonight that you need to learn what it truly means to serve your people as a leader. You need to understand what it takes to protect others. This is both your punishment and your training, Alex. You will join the Watch Guard alongside Dan."

Alex's face paled, but he didn't argue further. Dan felt a mixture of relief and apprehension. He would be free of his father's schemes, but at what cost to his already strained relationship with Alex?

As if on cue, a knock sounded at the door. The King called for entry, and Dan recognized the grizzled face of Watch Guard Quinn as he stepped into the room.

"Your Majesty," Quinn said with a bow. "The preparations are complete."

King Xandros nodded. "Good. Dan, Alex, you will go with Quinn now. Gather what you need for your journey to the Watch Tower. And Alex," he added, his tone softening slightly, "I hope you will use this time to reflect on your actions and your future responsibilities."

Alex's jaw clenched, but he nodded stiffly. As they were led from the room, Dan saw four guards waiting outside – two for each of them. There would be no escape, no last-minute reprieves.

As they walked through the dimly lit castle halls, Alex several paces ahead and flanked by his guards, Dan felt a strange mix of emotions. Fear of the unknown path ahead, relief at escaping his father's machinations, and a glimmer of hope for a future where he could make his own choices.

Quinn's gruff voice broke through Dan's thoughts. "You'll be staying in the guest quarters tonight. We leave for the Watch Tower at first light."

Dan nodded, realizing with a start that this would be his last night in Skycliff. The city he'd called home his entire life suddenly felt alien and distant.

When they reached the guest wing, Quinn directed them to separate rooms. Alex was ushered into his quarters without a word, the slam of his door echoing in the quiet hallway. Dan stood before his own assigned room, hesitating for a moment before stepping inside.

The room was simple but comfortable, a far cry from his chambers in the Torren estate. Dan sat heavily on the bed, the events of the night crashing over him in waves. He was free from his father's plots, but at what cost?

His thoughts turned to Leandra. Guilt and worry gnawed at him as he imagined his sister alone in their family home. Would she be all right without him? Their parents' manipulative and abusive nature had always been a shared burden, and now Leandra would have to bear it alone.

Dan paced the room, sleep feeling impossibly far away despite his exhaustion. He longed to send a message to Leandra, to explain, to warn her. But he knew any communication would be intercepted, potentially putting her in more danger.

"I'm sorry, Le-le," he whispered to the empty room. "Stay strong. Stay smart."

As the night deepened outside his window, Dan's mind raced with possibilities. Perhaps Leandra would find a way out too. She was clever, far more so than their parents realized. But the thought of leaving her behind still felt like a betrayal.

Dan flopped back onto the bed, staring at the unfamiliar ceiling. Tomorrow, he would leave for the Watch Tower, embarking on a path he'd never imagined for himself. But tonight, in this quiet room in Skycliff, he was caught between two worlds – the life he was leaving behind and the uncertain future ahead.

Sleep, when it finally came, was fitful and filled with dreams of shadowy figures and his sister's distant voice calling for help. Dan's last conscious thought before drifting off was a mix of hope and determination. Somehow, someday, he would find a way to help Leandra too. For now, all he could do was face the dawn and the new life that awaited him at the Watch Tower.

Chapter 12: Shattered Illusions

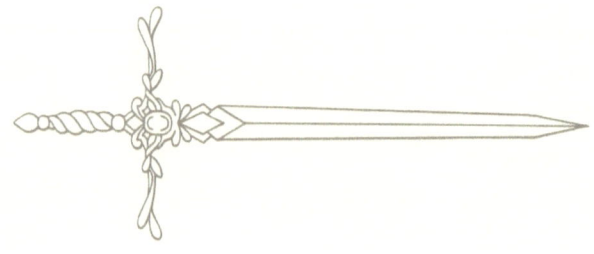

Leandra pressed herself against the cool stone wall, her heart racing. She had slipped away from the main gathering, desperate for a moment of solitude, only to stumble upon a conversation that chilled her to the bone.

"The Red Hand's operations in Skycliff are expanding," a hushed voice said. "The latest shipment of 'merchandise' arrived without incident."

"Excellent," another voice replied, one Leandra recognized as belonging to Lord Cavendish, a prominent noble. "And the Red House? No issues there?"

"None. The drugs keep them compliant. Chains for the troublesome ones."

Leandra's blood ran cold. Merchandise? Drugs? Chains? The implications were horrifying. The Red House wasn't just a place of ill repute — it was a prison for the enslaved.

As the conversation continued, Leandra's mind reeled. Names of noble families were mentioned, each apparently playing a role in the Red Hand's activities. Her stomach lurched as she heard her own family name.

"The Torrens have been particularly useful," Lord Cavendish said. "Their merchant connections provide excellent cover."

As if summoned by the mention, Leandra heard her father's booming laugh approaching. She pressed herself further into the shadows, praying she wouldn't be discovered.

"Ah, Cavendish!" Lord Torren's voice rang out. "Just the man I wanted to see. You'll be pleased to know I've arranged for another shipment of 'specialty goods' to come through with my next silk delivery. The Red Hand will be most satisfied."

Leandra felt sick. Her own father, bragging about his involvement in such heinous activities. She had known her parents were ambitious, even ruthless, but this? This was beyond anything she had imagined.

But the worst was yet to come. As Leandra stood frozen in her hiding place, the conversation took an even darker turn.

"By the way, Torren," Cavendish said, his voice lowered, "what became of that troublesome Sword Guard? Thorn, wasn't it?"

Leandra's heart nearly stopped at the mention of Thorn's name. She held her breath, straining to hear every word.

Her father's laugh was cold and cruel. "Ah, yes. Thorn. He was becoming far too inquisitive for his own good. But I found a... suitable solution."

"Oh?" Cavendish sounded intrigued.

"I had the Red Hand take care of him," Lord Torren said, a note of smug satisfaction in his voice. "He's been sent to the Dark Sisterhood as one of their... special prisoners."

Leandra had to clamp a hand over her mouth to stifle a gasp. The Dark Sisterhood — a name spoken only in whispers, a coven of witches from a distant land known for their blood magic.

"The Dark Sisterhood?" Cavendish sounded impressed and a little fearful. "That's... quite permanent."

"Indeed," Lord Torren agreed. "They'll drain every last drop of life from him for their rituals. A fitting end for someone who dared to interfere with our plans."

As the two men moved away, their voices fading into the general din of the gathering, Leandra remained rooted to the spot. Her mind was reeling, her heart shattered into a thousand pieces.

Thorn. Her mentor, her friend. The man who had seen her potential, who had taught her in secret, believing in her when no one else did. And her father had condemned him to a fate worse than death.

The weight of the revelations crashed over Leandra like a tidal wave. The Red Hand's true nature, her family's involvement, and now Thorn's horrifying fate — it was too much to bear.

Unable to remain in the suffocating confines of the castle any longer, Leandra fled. She moved swiftly through the corridors, barely aware of her surroundings, until she found herself outside in the cool night air.

In a secluded corner of the gardens, far from prying eyes, Leandra finally allowed herself to break down. She fell to her knees, her body wracked with silent sobs. The world she thought she knew had crumbled around her, revealing a nightmare she could never have imagined.

As she knelt there, surrounded by the sweet scent of night-blooming flowers that now seemed to mock the darkness in her heart, Leandra made a silent vow. She would find a way to stop the Red Hand. She would expose the corruption that ran through the noble houses of Skycliff.

But for now, in the quiet solitude of the garden, Leandra mourned. For Thorn, for the innocents trapped by the Red Hand, and for the last shreds of her own innocence, lost forever on this fateful night.

CHAPTER 13: THE PATH

Farrald leaned against a pillar in the grand hall, his mind still reeling from the night's events. The opulence of the Unity Gathering felt hollow now, a thin veneer over the corruption he had glimpsed. He was so lost in thought that he barely noticed Quinn's approach until the grizzled Watch Guard was right beside him.

"Farrald," Quinn's gravelly voice broke through his reverie. "There's been a change of plans. We're leaving earlier than expected."

Farrald straightened, surprise etched on his face. "How early?"

"Before dawn," Quinn replied, his expression unreadable. "I've got your kit ready. You'll sleep in the barracks tonight."

As the implications sank in, Farrald felt a mix of excitement and trepidation. "My father—"

"Already informed," Quinn cut in. "In fact, he's here to say goodbye."

As if on cue, Farrald spotted his father making his way through the crowd. His usually jovial face was set in serious lines, his eyes reflecting a mix of pride and concern.

"Son," Joseth said, clasping Farrald's shoulder. "I hear you're off on your new adventure sooner than we thought."

Farrald nodded, suddenly finding it hard to speak. Despite their differences, the reality of leaving his father behind was hitting him hard.

His father's grip tightened slightly. "I want you to know, I'm proud of you. The Watch Guard... it's important work. Noble work." He paused, his next words carefully chosen. "Perhaps even more so than being a Shepherd."

Farrald felt a familiar pang of frustration. Even now, his father couldn't quite let go of his hopes for Farrald's future. "Father, I—"

"I know, I know," his father said, raising a hand. "You have your own path to walk. But promise me you'll give this a real chance. The Watch Guard or the merchant guild — both are respectable callings. More... practical than the Shepherds."

Farrald saw the love in his father's eyes, the genuine desire for his son's success. It made the gulf between them all the more painful. "I promise to do my best, Father. Whatever path I end up on."

His father pulled him into a tight embrace. "That's all I ask, son. That's all I ask."

As they parted, Farrald felt the weight of expectations and farewells settling on his shoulders. Quinn, who had been standing a respectful distance away, stepped forward. "Time to go, lad. Say your goodbyes."

With a final nod to his father, Farrald turned to follow Quinn. As they made their way through the castle corridors, the reality of his situation began to sink in. He was leaving everything he knew behind, stepping into an uncertain future.

"Get some rest," Quinn said as they reached the barracks. "We leave at first light."

But as Farrald lay on the unfamiliar bed, sleep eluded him. The events of the night, the weight of his decision, the look in his father's eyes — it all swirled in his mind, refusing to let him rest.

Unable to bear the confines of the barracks any longer, Farrald slipped out into the night. His feet carried him to the castle gardens, a place he had always found peaceful during his visits to the capital.

As he rounded a corner, he spotted a figure kneeling in a secluded area, shoulders shaking with silent sobs. With a start, he recognized her — a noble girl he had noticed earlier whose name he had caught in a bit of overheard conversation, Leandra Torren.

For a moment, Farrald hesitated. He was a stranger to her, and clearly, she was in the midst of private grief. But something — perhaps the same instinct that had drawn him to the path of a Shepherd — wouldn't let him just walk away.

"My lady," he said softly, approaching slowly. "Are you alright?"

Leandra's head snapped up, her tear-stained face a mix of surprise and wariness. "Who are you?"

Farrald nodded, kneeling beside her but keeping a respectful distance. "Farrald. I'm a new recruit of the Watch Guard, bound to leave tomorrow, but I... I couldn't help but notice your distress. Is there anything I can do?"

Leandra laughed bitterly. "Unless you can undo the evils of the world and bring back those lost to darkness, I'm afraid not."

The pain in her voice resonated with the turmoil in Farrald's own heart. Without thinking, he did what came naturally to him — he bowed his head and began to pray.

"Lord of Light," he murmured, "we come before you with heavy hearts. The world is full of shadows we don't understand, pain we can't fathom. But we ask for your guidance, your comfort. For those lost in darkness, we pray for light. For those burdened by sorrow, we pray for solace."

As he prayed, he felt Leandra's surprise give way to a quiet acceptance. When he finished, he looked up to find her watching him with a mix of curiosity and something like hope.

"You're not just a Watch Guard recruit, are you?" she asked softly.

Farrald shook his head. "My heart lies with the Shepherds, though fate seems to have other plans for now."

Leandra nodded, understanding dawning in her eyes. "Thank you," she said simply. "I... I needed that more than I realized."

They sat in companionable silence for a moment, two souls finding brief solace in a world that suddenly seemed much darker and more complex than they had ever imagined.

Finally, Farrald stood. "I have to go. I leave at dawn with Watch Guard Quinn."

Leandra rose as well, wiping the last traces of tears from her face. "Safe travels, Farrald. And... thank you. For the prayer, for the company. I hope our paths cross again."

As Farrald made his way back to the barracks, his heart felt lighter despite the challenges ahead. He might not know what the future held, but he knew he would face it with faith, compassion, and the strength to help others — whether as a Watch Guard, a Shepherd, or whatever role the Lord of Light had in store for him.

Chapter 14: Pride and Punishment

The pounding on his door jolted Alex awake, each knock reverberating painfully through his skull. He groaned, burying his face deeper into the pillow.

"Up and at 'em, Your Highness," Quinn's gruff voice called through the door. "We're leaving in an hour."

Reality crashed over Alex like a bucket of ice water. It hadn't been a nightmare. He was really being sent away with the Watch Guard, like some common recruit. Anger and shame battled for dominance as he dragged himself out of bed.

His head throbbed, a reminder of the drug-laced drink from the night before. The memory of the Red House, of his own weakness, made his cheeks burn with humiliation. And Dan... the thought of his former friend only stoked the fires of his resentment.

As Alex dressed, he caught sight of his reflection in the mirror. The young man staring back at him looked pale, disheveled, a far cry from the proud prince he was supposed to be. He straightened his shoulders, forcing his features into a mask of cold indifference. He wouldn't give them the satisfaction of seeing him broken.

In the corridor, he found Dan and Quinn waiting. Alex brushed past them without a word, his silence a wall between them. Let them think what they wanted. He didn't need their pity or their judgment.

The walk to the stables was mercifully quiet, save for the sound of their boots on the cobblestones. As they approached, Alex felt a flicker of hope for the first time since his father's pronouncement. At least he'd have Stormwind, his loyal stallion, for companionship on this journey. The thought of long rides, the wind in his hair, brought a small measure of comfort.

As they entered the stables, Alex noticed a fourth figure already there - a young man with red hair, dressed in simple clothes, who was carefully saddling a horse. The stranger glanced up as they entered, his eyes widening slightly at the sight of Alex, but he quickly looked away, focusing on his task.

"Your mount," Quinn said, gesturing to a sturdy brown mare. "Daisy here will serve you well on the journey."

Alex stared at the horse in disbelief. "Where's Stormwind?" he demanded, breaking his self-imposed silence.

"The king thought it best you start fresh," Quinn replied, his tone leaving no room for argument. "Daisy's experienced and even-tempered. She'll be a good match for you."

Alex clenched his jaw, swallowing the torrent of protests that threatened to spill out. Of course. His father wouldn't even allow him this small comfort. Everything was being stripped away, piece by piece.

As Dan and Quinn prepared their own mounts, Alex approached Daisy. The mare regarded him with calm, brown eyes, so different from Stormwind's fiery gaze. He stroked her neck, the familiar motions of preparing for a ride bringing a semblance of normalcy to this surreal morning.

Out of the corner of his eye, Alex saw the red-haired young man finish saddling his horse and move to stand near Quinn, who gave him a brief nod. So, this stranger was part of their group too. Another witness to his humiliation.

Mounting up, Alex felt a spark of determination ignite within him. So they thought to humble him, to break his spirit? They would be sorely disappointed. He would show them all — his father, Dan, Quinn, this new recruit, every last person who doubted him — that he was more than capable. He didn't need their help or their approval.

As the others finished their preparations around him, Alex sat tall in the saddle, his eyes fixed on the road ahead. He pointedly ignored the concerned glances Dan kept throwing his way and the curious looks from the red-haired recruit. Let them think whatever they wanted of him. He would endure this "punishment," excel at whatever tasks they set before him, and return to claim his rightful place.

With each hoofbeat taking him further from Skycliff, Alex's resolve hardened. This wasn't an ending, he told himself. It was a beginning. And when he returned, they would all see just how wrong they had been to underestimate him.

Chapter 15: A Light in the Shadows

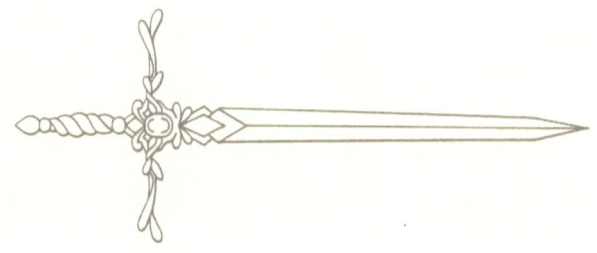

THE MOON HAD NOT yet sun, nor had the sun risen as Farrald led his horse, Buttercup, out of the stables. The mare nickered softly, seeming to share his mix of excitement and nervousness about the journey ahead.

As he waited for the others to join him, Farrald couldn't help but feel out of place. His simple, well-worn clothes stood in stark contrast to the fine attire of the two other young men with Quinn. He thought the blonde one was the one he had tried to help the night before, but he wasn't sure. While his clothes weren't as rich as the ones he had worn for the Unity gathering, they were still of much finer make than anything Farrald had ever seen. Both had family crests stitched onto their saddles and fine leather gambesons. Their bearing and the quality of their mounts also marked them as nobility, making Farrald acutely aware of his merchant's son background.

The sullen expressions on their faces puzzled him. Wasn't joining the Watch Guard an honor? Farrald's heart swelled with pride at the thought of serving, even if it wasn't the path he had initially chosen for himself.

"Good morning," Farrald ventured as the group assembled. "I'm Farrald. I look forward to training with you both."

The blonde-haired young man, who seemed about Farrald's age, merely grunted in response. The other, who had dark curly hair, gave a curt nod but remained silent. Quinn, noticing the awkward exchange, cleared his throat.

"Right, let's move out. Long journey ahead of us."

As they set off, the silence hanging over the group felt heavy and oppressive. Farrald tried once more to engage the one closer to his age in conversation.

"Have you trained with weapons before? I'm afraid I'm quite new to it all."

The young man's jaw tightened, and he urged his horse forward without a word. Farrald's shoulders slumped slightly. What had he done to offend them?

Realizing that his attempts at friendliness were unwelcome, Farrald decided to focus on the journey itself. He patted Buttercup's neck, grateful for her steady presence. As they rode through the awakening streets of Skycliff, Farrald let his mind wander to the challenge that lay ahead.

"Lord of Light," he prayed silently, "guide my steps on this new path. Grant me strength for the trials to come, and wisdom to serve with honor."

The familiar words of scripture came to his lips, a comforting rhythm that matched the steady clip-clop of the horses' hooves:

"Though the path be dark and treacherous,

I shall not falter, for You light my way.

In service to others, I find my purpose,

And in Your teachings, I find my strength."

As they passed through the city gates, Farrald's thoughts drifted to the young noblewoman he had met in the garden the night before. Leandra, with her tear-stained face and burden of unspoken sorrows. He hoped she would find solace in the days to come.

"Watch over Leandra, Lord," he prayed in an unvoiced whisper. "Ease her troubles and light her path, as You light mine."

The open road stretched before them, leading away from the only home Farrald had ever known. Yet instead of fear, he felt a growing sense of purpose. The Watch Guard might not have been his first choice, but he was determined to give it his all. Perhaps this was where the Lord of Light meant him to be, at least for now.

Farrald straightened in his saddle, a small smile playing on his lips despite the somber mood of his companions. The journey would be long, the training hard, but he was ready to face whatever challenges lay ahead. With faith as his shield and compassion as his sword, he would strive to be a beacon of light in the darkness, wherever his path might lead.

At the last gate, which went over a long bridge Quinn signaled for them to walk the horses. As the others dismounted, Farrald noticed an old woman sitting by the side of the road. She was hunched over, her weathered hands gripping a gnarled walking stick, her eyes squinting in the torchlight, which lit up the area.

Farrald approached the old woman. "Good day, grandmother," he said softly, kneeling beside her. "Are you alright? Do you need any assistance?"

The woman's rheumy eyes focused on him, a hint of surprise in their depths. "Bless you, young man," she croaked. "I'm just resting these old bones before continuing my journey."

Farrald nodded, offering a kind smile. "May I pray for you, grandmother? For strength and safety on your travels?"

At her nod, Farrald bowed his head. "Lord of Light, watch over this daughter of yours. Ease her aches, guide her steps, and bring her safely to her destination. May she find kindness and comfort along her way."

As he finished, he felt a gnarled hand pat his arm. "Thank you, child," the old woman said, her voice warmer now. "It's been long since anyone's shown such kindness to an old woman like me."

Farrald helped her to her feet, supporting her as she took a few tentative steps. "Safe travels, grandmother," he said, watching as she slowly made her way onto the bridge.

As he returned to the group, Farrald caught Quinn watching him, an unreadable expression on the older man's face. Dan and Alex, too, had paused in their tasks, their eyes following the old woman's receding figure.

No words were exchanged, but Farrald felt something shift in the air between them. It was subtle, barely perceptible, but it was there – a silent acknowledgment, perhaps, or a moment of shared humanity.

As they mounted up to continue their journey, Farrald sent up one last prayer. "Lord of Light, whatever lies ahead, help us face it together. Guide our steps, temper our fears, and open our hearts to one another."

With that, he urged his horse forward, ready to face whatever the road might bring. And though the silence remained, it felt just a little less heavy than before.

CHAPTER 16: WHISPERS OF CHANGE

THE FIRST LIGHT OF dawn had barely touched the sky when Leandra slipped out of her bed. She moved silently through the sleeping house, her heart pounding with a mixture of fear and determination. This was it—the moment she would take control of her destiny.

Donning her plainest dress, one that wouldn't draw attention in the bustling streets, Leandra made her way out of the Torren estate. The cool morning air filled her lungs as she walked briskly towards the castle, her mind racing with all she had to say.

At the castle gates, Leandra straightened her shoulders and addressed the guards with all the authority she could muster. "I seek an audience with King Xandros. I have urgent news regarding his son."

Her words had the desired effect. After a brief consultation, she was ushered inside and led through winding corridors to the King's private chambers. As she waited, Leandra took deep breaths, steeling herself for what was to come.

When King Xandros appeared, his eyes sharp despite the early hour, Leandra curtsied deeply. "Your Majesty, I thank you for seeing me. What I have to say concerns not only Prince Alex but the safety of the entire kingdom."

The King's eyebrow raised slightly, but he gestured for her to continue. Taking a deep breath, Leandra began to speak, her words tumbling out in a rush of pent-up fear and resolve.

She told him everything—the plot against Alex, the true nature of the Red House, the involvement of noble families, including her own parents, in the Red Hand's operations. As she spoke, she saw the King's expression darken, his hands clenching the arms of his chair.

"I want to help stop them, Your Majesty," Leandra said, her voice firm despite her racing heart. "I'm in a unique position to gather information, to thwart their schemes from within. But I need your support."

King Xandros leaned forward, his gaze intense. "What exactly are you proposing, Lady Leandra?"

"I ask that you assign a Sword Guard to work directly with me, someone we can both trust implicitly. I can convince my mother that I need protection if I'm to be courted by nobles for a marriage alliance. This would give me a trusted ally within our household, someone to pass information to and receive guidance from."

The King was silent for a long moment, considering her words. Finally, he nodded slowly. "Your bravery is commendable, Lady Leandra. And your plan... it has merit. Very well. I will assign my most trusted Sword Guard to this task. Theran will work with you, under the guise you suggested."

Leandra's heart skipped a beat at the mention of Theran's name. She hoped the flush she felt rising to her cheeks wasn't visible. "Thank you, Your Majesty. I won't let you down."

King Xandros leaned back in his chair, his expression softening slightly. "There's something else you should know, Lady Leandra. Your brother, Dan, left Skycliff early this morning."

Leandra's eyes widened in surprise. "Left? Where has he gone?"

"He has joined the Watch Guard," the King explained. "Along with my son, Alex, and another young recruit named Farrald. I felt it was necessary for Alex to... broaden his horizons, shall we say. Your brother's actions, while misguided at times, showed a strength of character that I believe will serve him well in the Watch Guard."

Leandra absorbed this information, a mix of relief and concern washing over her. "I... I see. Thank you for telling me, Your Majesty. I hope they will find strength in each other's company."

The King nodded. "As do I. The path ahead will not be easy for any of them, but I believe it's necessary. Just as the task I'm entrusting to you is necessary, Lady Leandra. We all have our parts to play in the days to come."

"Indeed, Your Majesty," Leandra agreed, her resolve strengthening. "And I am ready to play mine."

As she left the King's presence, her mind was already racing with plans and possibilities. She slipped back into the Torren estate just as the household was beginning to stir, her absence unnoticed.

In her room, Leandra allowed herself a small smile of triumph. She had taken the first step on a dangerous path, but one that could save countless lives. She was uniquely positioned to stop the Red Hand, to unravel the web of corruption that threatened the kingdom.

Her thoughts turned to Dan, now on his way to the Watch Guard with Farrald and Alex. She hoped her brother would find friendship with them, that he would treat both the gentle Farrald and the proud prince with equal kindness. They would all need allies in the days to come.

As for her parents... Leandra's smile turned grim. She would play the dutiful daughter, the perfect pawn in their games. But all the while, she would be working against them, manipulating them into revealing their secrets, using every skill they had taught her against them.

The sun was fully risen now, bathing her room in golden light. Leandra stood tall, feeling the weight of her new purpose settle on her shoulders. The road ahead would be fraught with danger, filled with secrets and lies. But she was ready. For Dan, for Alex, for Farrald, for Theran, for all those trapped by the Red Hand's cruelty—she would fight. And she would win.

Before the Torren household came to life around her, Leandra took a deep breath and prepared to step into her role. The game had begun.

***

The house was quiet, servants not yet stirring, her parents still asleep. This was her chance. Before anyone began to suspect her.

Heart pounding, she made her way to her father's study. The door was locked, of course, but Leandra had come prepared. From her sleeve, she produced a slender pick—a gift from Thorn during one of their clandestine lessons. "Knowledge is power," he had told her, "and sometimes, knowledge lies behind locked doors."

With trembling hands, she worked the lock. After a tense moment that felt like an eternity, she heard a soft click. Taking a deep breath, Leandra eased the door open and slipped inside.

The study was dark, heavy curtains blocking out the early morning light. Leandra didn't dare light a lamp. Instead, she relied on the faint glow from the hallway and her memory of the room's layout.

Her father's massive oak desk dominated the space. Leandra approached it cautiously, her eyes scanning for anything out of place. A stack of papers caught her attention—correspondence her father had been reading the night before.

With nimble fingers, she began to sift through the documents. Most were mundane—trade agreements, social invitations, petitions from lesser nobles. But near the bottom of the stack, a letter bearing an unfamiliar seal made her pause.

The seal was black wax, impressed with the image of a grasping hand. The Red Hand. Leandra's breath caught in her throat as she carefully unfolded the parchment.

The letter was written in code, but Leandra recognized a few key phrases from conversations she'd overheard. "Shipment," "Red House," "royal leverage." This was exactly the kind of information the King needed.

Leandra pulled a small notebook from her pocket. In her own cipher—one she and the King had agreed upon—she jotted down what she could decipher from the letter. Her hand shook slightly, but her writing remained steady.

Just as she finished, a floorboard creaked in the hallway outside. Leandra froze, her heart hammering in her chest. Had her father awakened early?

After a moment of terrifying silence, she heard the shuffle of feet moving away. Probably a servant beginning their morning routine.

Leandra let out a shaky breath. It was time to go. She carefully replaced the papers exactly as she'd found them, tucking her notebook securely in her bodice. With one last scan of the room to ensure everything was in place, she slipped back out into the hallway, locking the door behind her.

As she hurried back to her room, Leandra's mind raced. She had done it—her first real act of espionage. The thrill of success warred with the weight of her new responsibility. This was no game; lives hung in the balance.

Back in the safety of her chambers, Leandra pulled out her notebook. She had to get this information to the King as soon as possible. But how?

Then she remembered—her mother had asked her to send a letter to a dressmaker in the city. It was the perfect cover.

Leandra began to write, her pen flying across the paper. To anyone else, it would appear to be a simple request for a new gown. But hidden within the innocuous words about fabrics and fittings was the vital information she'd uncovered.

As she sealed the letter, Leandra felt a mix of pride and trepidation. There was no going back now. She had taken her first true step down this dangerous path.

"For you, Thorn," she whispered, touching the seal. "For Dan, for Alex, for all those the Red Hand would harm. I will not fail."

With that, she rang for a servant. It was time to set her message in motion—and to begin her day as Lady Leandra Torren, dutiful daughter and secret agent of the King.

Chapter 17: The Road Ahead

THE SUN HAD CRESTED the horizon when Dan realized the familiar walls of Skycliff were receding behind him. The cobblestone streets gave way to a dirt road, each hoofbeat carrying him further from the only life he'd ever known. He couldn't help but twist in his saddle, stealing one last glance at the city that had been his home.

Skycliff's towers pierced the morning mist, the golden light of dawn painting them in hues of amber and rose. The sight stirred a complex mix of emotions in Dan's chest – relief, regret, fear, and a strange sense of loss. For all its flaws, for all the pain and manipulation he'd endured there, it was still home.

"Eyes forward, lad," Quinn's gruff voice cut through Dan's reverie. "What's behind you is gone. Best focus on what's ahead."

Dan turned back, his cheeks burning with embarrassment. Quinn was right, of course. There was no going back now. Whatever lay ahead – the rigors of Watch Guard training, the mysteries of ancient weapons, the looming threat of the Red Hand – that was his future now.

His gaze drifted to his companions. Alex rode slightly ahead, his back rigid, eyes fixed firmly on the road before them. The anger radiating from the prince was palpable, a stark reminder of how far their friendship had fallen. Dan's heart ached at the memory of simpler times, of shared laughter and dreams of adventure. Now, those memories felt like relics from another life entirely.

Farrald, the red-haired recruit, rode to Dan's left. There was an earnest-ness about him that Dan found both admirable and slightly discomfiting. In another time, another place, perhaps they could have been friends. But here, now, with the weight of recent events pressing down on him, Dan found himself at a loss for words.

As they rode on, the landscape began to change. The manicured gardens and grand estates of Skycliff's outskirts gave way to rolling hills and verdant forests. They were entering the Forest District, a place Dan had only heard about in passing conversations at court.

To his surprise, the forest was nothing like the dark, forbidding woods of his imagination. Sunlight filtered through the canopy, dappling the forest floor with warm patches of light. The air was fresh and clean, filled with the scent of pine and wildflowers. As they traveled deeper into the district, Dan began to notice signs of life – small cottages nestled among the trees, smoke rising from chimneys, the distant laughter of children at play.

It was a world away from the life he'd known in Skycliff. Here, there were no whispered conspiracies in shadowy corridors, no constant ma-neuvering for political advantage. Just people living their lives, tending their farms, raising their families. The simplicity of it all was both foreign and deeply appealing to Dan.

As they passed through a small village, Dan found himself captivated by the sights and sounds of everyday life. A blacksmith hammered away at his forge, the rhythmic clanging echoing through the air. Children chased each other through the streets, their faces free from the carefully cultivated masks that noble children learned to wear from an early age. In the village square, farmers haggled good-naturedly over the price of vegetables, their interactions a far cry from the veiled barbs and subtle threats that passed for conversation in Skycliff's court.

Dan felt a pang of envy. How different might his life have been if he'd been born here, among these people? To live without the constant weight of expectations and political machinations, to be judged solely on one's own merits and actions – it seemed like a dream.

But as they rode on, leaving the village behind, Dan's thoughts turned to the challenges that lay ahead. The life of a Watch Guard was far from simple or easy. Quinn's weathered face and alert eyes were testament to the hardships and dangers they would face.

What would it take to succeed in this new life? Dan began to make a mental list of the skills he'd need to develop. Swordsmanship, of course – he'd had some training, but he knew it was nothing compared to the martial prowess of a true Watch Guard. He'd need to build his strength and endurance, learn to track and hunt, to survive in the wilderness. And there would be other skills too, he was sure – skills he couldn't even imagine yet.

Beyond the physical challenges, Dan knew he'd need to work on himself as well. The political acumen he'd developed in Skycliff's court might serve him well in some ways, but he'd need to learn to be more direct, more honest. The Watch Guard had no place for the kind of subtle manipulations and hidden agendas that were second nature in noble circles.

And then there were the ancient weapons – the blades of power that featured so prominently in tales of the Watch Guard's greatest deeds. Dan's hand unconsciously drifted to the hilt of his own sword, an ordinary blade that suddenly felt inadequate. He knew such weapons were typically reserved for the Sword Guard of the Triune Halls, but a small part of him dared to hope. If he worked hard enough, proved himself worthy enough, might he one day be entrusted with such a weapon?

The thought filled him with a mixture of excitement and trepidation. To wield a blade of power against the Red Hand, to strike a decisive blow against the darkness that threatened the kingdoms – it was a heady prospect. But with such power would come immense responsibility. Was he ready for that? Could he ever be?

As the day wore on and the miles passed beneath their horses' hooves, Dan found his resolve strengthening. The doubts and fears that had plagued him since leaving Skycliff didn't vanish, but they receded, replaced by a growing sense of purpose. This was his chance to become something more than a pawn in someone else's game. To make a real difference in the world.

He glanced at his companions – Quinn's steady presence, Farrald's wide-eyed determination, and Alex's rigid back. Whatever lay ahead, they would face it together. And maybe, just maybe, they would emerge on the other side as something greater than they had been before.

As the sun began to dip towards the horizon, painting the sky in brilliant shades of orange and purple, Dan felt a glimmer of hope. The road ahead was long and undoubtedly fraught with challenges. But for the first time in a long while, he felt truly free. Free to shape his own destiny, to become the kind of person he'd always aspired to be.

With one last look at the fading light of day, Dan set his eyes on the path ahead. His new life as a Watch Guard recruit had begun, and he was determined to make the most of it. Whatever came next, he would face it head-on, with courage and determination. The boy who had left Skycliff that morning was already fading away, and in his place, a new Dan was emerging – one ready to face the challenges of the Watch Guard and beyond.

***

The sun hung low in the sky, casting long shadows across the road as Quinn called for a halt. They had been riding for hours, and both horses and riders needed rest. As they dismounted near a small stream, Dan felt the weight of the day's journey in his bones.

While the others tended to the horses, Dan found himself a quiet spot by the roadside. He sat on a fallen log, his mind swirling with the events of the past day and the uncertain future that lay ahead. Almost unconsciously, his hand went to his neck, fingers finding the small, familiar shape that hung there.

The pendant was silver, intricately carved with the Torren family crest. His father had given it to him on his sixteenth birthday, a symbol of his place in the family and the expectations that came with it. Dan had worn it every day since, a constant reminder of who he was and where he came from.

Now, as he held it in his palm, the pendant felt heavier than ever. It was beautiful, valuable – and a chain tying him to a life he was leaving behind.

Dan stood, the pendant clutched tightly in his fist. He took a few steps away from the group, to the very edge of the road. For a long moment, he simply stared at the small silver object, memories flashing through his mind – some good, many painful, all part of a past he could no longer cling to.

"Everything alright, lad?" Quinn's voice carried from where he was watering the horses.

Dan took a deep breath. "Yes," he called back, surprised to find he meant it. "Just... saying goodbye to something."

With that, he knelt down and gently placed the pendant on a flat rock by the roadside. The silver gleamed in the fading sunlight, catching the eye. Someone would find it, Dan knew. A traveler, a merchant, perhaps a child from a nearby farm. To them, it would be a stroke of luck, a valuable trinket to sell or trade. To Dan, it was the cutting of a final tie to his old life.

As he stood, Dan felt lighter, as if a weight he hadn't fully realized he'd been carrying had been lifted from his shoulders. He was no longer Dan Torren, scion of a noble house, pawn in political games. He was just Dan, Watch Guard recruit, forging his own path.

He turned back to the group, noting the curious glances from Farrald and the studiously ignored look from Alex. Quinn merely nodded, a glimmer of understanding in his weathered features.

"Ready to move on?" the old soldier asked.

Dan squared his shoulders, feeling a new resolve settle over him. "Yes," he said firmly. "I'm ready."

As they prepared to mount up, Quinn's gaze swept over the group - Dan with his newfound determination, Alex's barely concealed resentment, and Farrald's earnest attention. The old soldier's weathered face softened slightly.

"Listen up, all of you," Quinn said, his gruff voice carrying a note of seriousness that caught everyone's attention. "I know you've all got your differences. Royal, noble, merchant's son - doesn't matter out here. What matters is that we work together."

He paused, making sure he had each of their eyes. "The path ahead isn't easy. The Watch Guard demands everything you've got, and then some. But if you learn to rely on each other, to be stronger as a whole, you'll find you're capable of more than you ever thought possible."

The words hung in the air, heavy with meaning. Dan saw Farrald nod earnestly, while Alex's scowl deepened, though there was a flicker of something - consideration, perhaps - in his eyes.

Quinn mounted his horse with the ease of long practice. "Now, let's move out. We've got a long road ahead."

As they set off once more, Dan felt a mix of emotions swirling within him. The weight of the discarded pendant was gone, replaced by the challenge of Quinn's words. Working together wouldn't be easy, not with the tensions that simmered between them. But as the road stretched out before them, leading into the gathering dusk, Dan felt a glimmer of hope.

He urged his horse forward, ready to meet whatever lay ahead. The past was behind him now, left by the roadside like the silver pendant. Ahead lay a future full of challenges, but also of possibility. And for the first time in a long while, Dan felt truly ready to face it - not alone, but as part of something larger than himself.

The group rode on, a trainer and three disparate individuals, with an uncertain future together for a time. What the Watch Guard would hold for each of them, only time would tell. But as the last light of day faded and the first stars began to twinkle overhead, Dan couldn't help but feel they were riding towards something that would change their lives.

GLOSSARY

Main Cast of Characters:
   Dan Torren: Nobleman's son,
   Leandra Torren: Dan's sister
   Alex: Crown Prince of Septily
   Farrald: Merchant's son
   Quinn: Experienced member of the Watch Guard

Supporting Cast of Characters:
King Xandros: Ruler of Septily, Alex's father
Lord Torren: Dan and Leandra's father, involved with the Red Hand
Lady Torren: Dan and Leandra's mother
Thorn: Former Sword Guard, Leandra's mentor, missing
Theran: a Sword Guard, personal guard for King Xandros
Callum Harnen: a young noble friend of Alex
Rowan Harnen: a young noble friend of Alex
Zara: Sword Guard, part of Alex's personal guard
Captain Oren: Sword Guard captain mentioned by Zara
Lord Cavendish: a noble
Joseth: Farrald's father, a merchant from the Desert District.
Juliay: One Farrald's friends from home (mentioned but not seen)
Shepherd Jordan: Seen leaving the Unity Gathering with Theran.
.

Places/Geography:
Septily: The kingdom where the story takes place
Skycliff: The capital city of Septily

Forest District: An area outside Skycliff with small villages and farm-
land

Red House: Illegal brothel in Skycliff, linked to the Red Hand

Watch Tower: Destination of the Watch Guard recruits (mentioned
but not visited in the novella)

Desert District: Farrald's home region

Entities and Organizations:

The Red Hand: A shadowy organization of merchants, mercenaries,
and witches involved in illegal activities

Watch Guard: An elite, interkingdom peacekeeping group, guarding
ancient weapons and knowledge

Triune Halls: The three branches of service in Septily

*Sword Guards: Elite warriors and protectors

*Shepherds: Spiritual guides and healers

*Lawgivers: Judges and administrators of the law

Dark Sisterhood: A coven of witches from another country who practice blood magic

Noble Houses: The ruling families of Septily, including the Torrens

Key Concepts:

Blades of Power: Ancient weapons

Unity Gathering: A celebration bringing together nobles and members
of the Triune Halls

Lord of Light: The deity Farrald worships

MORE TO READ IN THE WORLD OF ARAMATIR

I hope you enjoyed this introduction to *The Dark Blade Trilogy*! *Dark Blade Forged* is currently available where most books are sold online and available for order for brick-and-mortar bookstores.

Dark Blade Tempered (Book 2 in The Dark Blade Trilogy) will be coming in spring of 2025, with Dark Blade Sharpened coming out after that.

If you enjoy the world of Aramatir, The Champion Trilogy is the first fantasy trilogy I wrote and published and is based in Aramatir.

Dark Blade Forged Excerpt

Dark Blade Forged

Series: The Dark Blade Trilogy, Vol. 1

ISBN: 979-8-9870648-6-3   ASIN: 979-8-9870648-4-9

Word Count: 93k

In a world where ancient powers stir and darkness threatens, Dan Torren seeks to escape his noble family's corruption by joining the mysterious WatchGuard. As Dan and his allies uncover a sinister plot involving the Red Hand, an organization trafficking in human lives, Dan will need to confront his own inner desire for vengeance.

When he discovers a legendary and strangely shadowy blade, he's thrust into a destiny greater than he ever imagined. Alongside his friends—Alex, a conflicted prince, and Farrald, a would-be Shepherd—Dan must navigate political intrigue, confront dark forces, and face his own family's twisted legacy.

Dan's journey will challenge everythinghe believes about justice, power, and his own identity. With the fate ofSeptily hanging in the balance, can Dan forge a new path for justice?

Dark Blade Forged is a gripping Christian Fantasy tale of friendship, betrayal, and the price of power in a world where the lines between good and evil blur with every choice.

Excerpt from the middle of the book:

The tug brought Dan to a door carved with several figures. The tautness of the pull intensified again him as he swept away the dirt over the carving. The figures on the door were old Champions. He could tell by the familiarity of some likenesses found in some places in Skycliff, although others weren't as familiar to him. The group of Champions surrounded a single box in which a shattered blade rested. The carving was intricate, and Dan ran his fingers over the shattered blade, and then opened the door.

Inside, he could see the box from the carving. It was an iron trunk with a strange padlock. The grooves of a handprint layover the top of the lock. Sand, dust, and mist swirled around the trunk, butDan moved toward it.

Behind Dan, Terese murmured something, but hedid not make out the words. Consumed now by the need to open that box, heplaced his hand over the handprint. A rational part of his brain wanted him tostop, but the compulsion moved him forward, despite the unlikelihood of hishand fitting the handprint.

His hand fit perfectly in the grooves. A glowemanated around his fingers, but it was not a glow of light, but of texturedshadow, a shimmering black that seemed deeper than even the dark shadows of thechamber beyond the light from Terese's blade.

An audible click resonated through his hand, his chest, and the chamber, and the lock fell open. With trembling hands, Dan opened the lid of the iron box and gazed down at the broken blade within. It was shimmering obsidian, alive with power from within each of the seven, jagged pieces. Dan ran his fingers carefully over the tip of the top piece of the glowing shards, feeling a sensation of warmth and power running from his hands to his heart. He couldn't let this blade lay here unused any longer. He touched each of the seven shards, traced his hands over the engravings on the cross guard, and then reached for the hilt.

As his fingers came around the leather-wrapped grip, a heavy, warm wave rushed through him, from somewhere within his fingertips to the hilt, and somehow, resonated in ripples through the shattered pieces of the sword which began to melt and reshape.

In the deepest recesses of his mind, Dan wanted to let go of the blade, but he did not. He held fast as it took shape in front of him, perfectly balanced for his hand, for the extension of his arm. It was a part of him, and it was hungry for justice, for vengeance, for righteousness against those who would do harm to his people, and peace for those who would live with kindness. It opened up parts of him he had closed off, even from his own thoughts, and he felt as if a part of him had been hollowed out and refilled, then hollowed and filled again.

Buy Links: Updated Universal Link

About the Author

Tyrean Martinson recognizes she has an unusual name. Tyrean can be pronounced many different ways (and has been) but her parents liked the idea of not having two "e" letters in her name but pronouncing it "Tyrene". She has lived in Washington State her entire life but loves to travel in the US and internationally. The daughter and granddaughter of avid readers and storytellers, Tyrean has loved the landscape of Story for as long as she can remember. She told her first stories to her dog and her cat and entered a classroom short story contest in sixth grade. While she didn't win, she did receive encouragement from her teacher who said, "You could become an author." Astounded that this was possible, she began to fill notebooks with ideas, daydreams, and more. Years passed, life happened, and experience was gained. Tyrean is the author of over twenty books, over a hundred published poems, and dozens of published short stories. She also enjoys hearing all the stories her husband and daughters have to tell her about their everyday lives because they inspire her to write with courage.

Also by

To read any of the following books, you can find links here:
Tyrean's Link List

In the World of Aramatir
Dark Blade: Forged (prequel to The Champion Trilogy)

In the Champion Trilogy:
Champion in the Darkness
Champion in Flight
Champion's Destiny

In the Universe of Anomalies
The Rayatana Series
Liftoff
Nexus

Collections of Short Stories and Poetry
Dragonfold and Other Adventures
Flicker: A Collection of Short Stories and Poetry
Light Reflections
Microfiction Multiverse (Forthcoming)

Non-Fiction
A Pocket-Sized Jumble of 500+ Writing Prompts
Jumble Journal 1
Jumble Journal 2
5… 4… 3… 2… 1… Write: 25 Speculative Fiction Writing Prompts
Dynamic Writing 1
Dynamic Writing 2
Dynamic Writing 3

Devotionals
Summer Devotions
Walking with Jesus: Stories from One Hope Church (as the editor and a contributing author)

Short Ebook Titles and Experimental Fiction
Ashes Burn: Seasons 1-7, Micro-Fiction Series as an Ebook
Seedling, a flash fiction reprint ebook
The Story Addict

Tyrean is featured in the following anthologies:
Hero Lost: Mysteries of Death and Life, a IWSG Anthology of Fantasy
Book to Dreams 1
Creative Colloquy 7
Best of Every Day Poets 1
Best of Every Day Poets 2
Overcoming Adversity: An Anthology for Andrew
The Insecure Writer's Support Group Guide to Publishing and Beyond
The Insecure Writer's Support Group Writing for Profit
Sunday Snaps: The Stories
New Voices IV: A Commercial Fiction Anthology